ALONE

IN THE PIRATES' LAIR.

REPRINTED FROM THE "BOYS OF ENGLAND" JOURNAL.

BEAUTIFULLY ILLUSTRATED.

PUBLISHING OFFICE, 173, FLEET STREET, E.C.

MDCCCLXX.

ALONE IN THE PIRATES' LAIR.

"HIS FINGERS TOUCH THE PISTOL—THE PIRATE EMITS A DEEP, FIERCE GROWL."

CHAPTER I.

HOMEWARD BOUND.

The good ship "Titania," homeward bound from Canton, and laden with a costly cargo, lies at anchor off the Ladrones.

Leaning lightly against the taffrail, a young midshipman gazed dreamingly through the glowing, limitless expanse of blending sky and sea.

"Aha! here it comes at last!"

The boy started, and looked round inquiringly.

The first mate, who had stepped to his side unobserved by him, uttered this exclamation in a tone of intense satisfaction.

"Aye, sir; in yonder cloud to starboard?"

"Yes, Mr. Rushton, that little cloud, not bigger than a man's hand, and soon we shall have it in right earnest; be so good as to call the captain."

"Aye, sir," returned the mid, touching his cap respectfully.

He stepped nimbly from the quarterdeck, went below, and tapped at the captain's door.

"Come in."

The boy entered.

"Wind, Mr. Rushton?"

"Aye, sir."

"Which way?"

"North-west and by north, sir."

"Good! tell Mr. Dale to heave anchor at once; I'll be on deck in a few moments."

"Aye, sir."

Soon the boatswain's whistle rung shrilly along the quiet deck.

The crew came tumbling up the hatchways, or sprung from the forecastle and from under the bulwarks.

"All hands up anchor, ahoy!" was the boatswain's gruff shout.

The fifer struck up a jaunty air.

"Man the bars!"

And then came the order,

"Heave around!"

Forty sturdy tars tramped, tramped, tramped around, their broad, brawny shoulders bearing hard against the capstan-bars, and their bare, light-tripping feet keeping smart time to the squealing notes of the pipe.

> "Yo-ho, heave-ho, jolly hearts,
>   With a heave yho!
> Yo-ho, heave-ho, jolly hearts,
>   And away we go!
>   Heave yho!"

The captain came on deck and advanced towards the lieutenant.

They exchanged a salute.

"Time we were moving, Mr. Dale."

"Aye, sir," returned the other, with a smile; "the men were grumbling this morning, and swore, as usual, that we were aground on our own beef-bones."

"Humph! but there's an ugly frown northward; we shall have a squall, I fear."

"Wind freshens already, sir."

"Well, we can make a good offing."

"We're short!" shouted a voice.

The ship was nearly over her anchor.

"Heave and fall!" cried the lieutenant.

Then, after a pause, the word was given to "Heave away."

Once more, to the shrill music of the pipe, the men tramped around and around the capstan.

The anchor was upheaved.

The sails loosened and bellied out before the rising wind.

When all was ready, fore and aft, the officer gave the command—

"Let fall!"

And the good ship was once more under way.

Soaring nobly under a cloud of canvas, the ship travelled bravely onwards through the shimmering foam.

The captain and the first mate went below.

The young mid leaped upon the rattlins.

Of the sun's disc only the red rim remained above the molten waters, haloed by a softened amber glow.

At last the red-hot ring dwindled away into one fiery spark, burnt fiercely for a few moments, and then quenched out in the darkened ocean.

It was an august, a glorious spectacle, as the boy hung lightly in the fore rigging and gazed above and below.

Jack Rushton was a handsome, manly lad, about fourteen years old; he had frank, blue eyes and fair hair; he was merry as a lark, agile as a monkey, and brave as the aweless lion.

Jack's mother was the widow of a naval officer; he had no brothers or sisters, and inherited nothing from his parents but their good looks, sterling virtues, and self-reliance.

He ran nimbly down the rigging, and lightly sprang upon deck.

He walked aft.

A group, consisting of the boatswain, a negro servant, and a fairy little girl, the captain's daughter, stood by the lee-bulwark, gazing upon the starlit sky and glimmering main.

"Oh! lift me now right up, Uncle Pomp. I want to see them shining in the water," said the little girl, laying her tiny white fingers on the African's big, black hand, and keeping her eyes fixed wonderingly upon the brilliant Southern Cross which glittered far across the blue heavens.

The negro uttered a chuckling laugh, and raised the little girl high in his sturdy arms.

Uttering a gleeful cry she clapped her little white hands together.

Her large, pensive, blue eyes dilated, and a sigh fluttered from her arched lips.

"Ah me! so beautiful!" she murmured.

"Eh! Why fo' yo sigh, lilly missee?"

"Oh! Uncle Pomp, if I could fly," continued the child, with a bound, heavenward. "If I had fine strong wings like the frigate-bird papa showed us, to fly up, and up, and far, far away, among all those twinkling stars, I should never want to come down here any more."

"Oh! dat nebba, nebba do. 'Pears yo bery curis, lilly missee; 'pose yo fly away? What pa do? What ole Pomp do?"

"And old Tom Hawser?" rejoined the bo'swain, in his gruff but good-humoured voice.

"Yah! break um 'art. What for yo fly away, eh? 'Pose yo fall in de sea, one darned ole shark ab yo. Go 'long. Lilly missee muss 'top wid ole Pomp, he de boy to take care ob she——

"'Nebba fly away,
Dat would nebba do;
Buccra cap'en break um 'art,
Pomp um break um too.'

"Yah!"

Like the gush of fairy bells the pretty child's light laugh rang sweetly along the silent deck.

"Who talks of flying away?" was asked in a deep, manly voice by some one, who, at the moment, stepped from the after-hatch. "My Nellie! What! and leave me? Fie!"

"You, dear papa, no—never!" murmured the girl, springing into her father's arms. "Please let me stay with you always."

The captain smoothed her flaxen curls, and raised her on to his broad shoulder.

She wove her little smooth arms coaxingly round his neck, and rested her golden brow among his dark hair.

Still she kept her glance fixed on the silvern blaze in the blue vault above.

"Papa," she whispered softly.

"Well, my pet?"

"The floor of heaven!" murmured the little one. "When we were at our house, you know, Nurse Hester used to tell me, papa, *that* was the floor of heaven; so mamma is gone up yonder, and I think she looks down upon us now, and knows that we are out on the lonely seas such a long, long way from home. Mamma seems speaking to me now."

A shade of anguish for an instant darkened the captain's brow.

He drew his little daughter down to his breast, and clutched her tightly there.

Then he set her on her feet, and took her by the hand.

"Come, Nell, you'll take cold, my birdie," he said. "Let us go below."

The boatswain had withdrawn to a respectful distance, and stood looking on complacently.

"Who takes the trick for the dog-watch?" asked the captain; "you, Mr. Rushton?"

"Aye, sir," responded our hero, touching his cap.

"Keep a sharp look out. Hawser?"

"Here, sir."

"Keep her up to the wind; but should it blow half a gale, call me."

The captain and his little daughter retired.

The negro followed.

The boatswain issued certain orders to the watch, and then, with the young mid, walked forward.

The elder seaman took a seat on a carronade slide, and slipping a quid into his cheek, seemed to be ruminating profoundly.

"In the doldrums, Mr. Hawser?" asked our friend Jack, with a laugh.

Mr. Hawser made no reply, but began to whistle "Hearts of Oak," and then, as if the liveliness of that tune jarred with the sombreness of his mood, changed it for "All in the Downs."

Jack ventured another remark.

"Glad she travels at last; I've had enough of lying abreast that bit of reef, with the sun bleaching the decks, and bronzing our figure-heads, for I'm getting homesick, and shall be glad to see the Lizard once more."

"Shiver my timbers—saving your presence, Mr. Rushton—but I wish a safe landfall to all poor souls aboard this here same blessed wessel," grunted the boatswain, with unwonted vehemence, "for, blow me, sir, if there hasn't been, since we hoisted the blue peter, under sailin' orders, foretokens enough to sink a three-decker."

"Foretokens? What do you mean, Mr. Hawser?"

"Call me a lubber, sir, if I haven't had 'em myself."

"Oh, presentiments of evil."

"Belay all that, sir; my *sentiments* are no more evil than those of another," grumbled the old tar.

"You mistake, indeed, Mr. Hawser," said Jack; "everyone aboard respects you, and knows you to be——"

"Avast! It may be so, or it may not be so; but if there's anything I hate wuss than insiniwations, it's palavering. But, hark ye, Mr. Rushton, didn't we set sail on Friday?"

"What then?"

"Pah!"

"And so far, excepting a few days' dead calm, we have had a merry cruise."

"So far! humph! And then Miss Nell's pussy-cat——"

"Fell overboard."

"My limbs, Mr. Rushton, what—have—you—got—to—say—arter—that bad omen?"

"It was a sad cat—astrophe."

"Ah! and then the captain's little cherub; didn't ye mark how she up-turned her pretty peepers to the stars, and talked about flying away, as if she knew what were coming?"

"Mere child-like feeling."

The boatswain groaned his disgust at Jack's unbelief, and rose impatiently.

"Mark my words, Mr. Rushton," he grumbled, "I may be a big lubber with no more top-hamper than would serve a lop-lolly-boy to p'ison a monkey, but ——"

"No, no."

"Werry good, Mr. Rushton, and this is all betwixt ourselves and the main-m'st. I say as if *this same vessel don't founder in a tornado she'll run athwart hawse with a pirate!*"

With this prediction, Tom Hawser vanished down the main hatchway.

Left alone, Jack paced the deck, keeping his lonely watch with due vigilance.

Glancing astern, he perceived a vast pall of dense black cloud slowly rising along the horizon blotting dead out the glittering stars, and merging the sky line in a broad span of inky darkness.

Still slowly, but surely, rose that black pall.

The sails flapped, as the wind veered, then the ship lurched; again the sails swelled out, and the waves bowled against her taut sides in heavier masses.

Soon the whole heavens were curtained in impenetrable gloom.

The lights aboard, which before had

shown sickly faint in the brilliant star-shine, now glimmered with their fullest brightness.

But the darkness enshrouded the travelling ship like a thick, black mist.

After an hour the wind fell.

The ship quivered, and seemed taken aback. Jack looked over the side.

Profound darkness; save that aft a bright yellow gleam shot from the open dead-light of the captain's cabin.

Jack resumed his walk along the deck.

The weary minutes lagged on.

Again the wind fell.

Jack struck a match.

The little blue bead of light broke into a long flare, and burnt steadily.

Jack muttered an exclamation of impatience, and was about to call, when suddenly a stern, loud voice shouted through the gloom—

"All hands on deck! Lower the peak; slack away the main halyards; in mainsail; clue up, and furl everything but the top'sails. Bo'swain, ahoy!"

CHAPTER II.

THE WHITE SQUALL.

THE crew, who had crowded on deck at the stern, loud summons of the first-lieutenant, seconded by the sonorous roar of the boatswain's trumpet, rushed about in seeming confusion. The sharp yell of the men stationed in the tops, the roaring of the boatswain, the deep, manly shouts of the first-mate, the shrill, boyish cries of the midshipmen, the rattling of blocks and cordage, mingled in mighty uproar.

The noble-looking captain took his stand upon the main-gangway and issued his skilled orders in tones clear, distinct, and calm.

And what was the cause of this sudden commotion?

Look astern.

All darkness! No—what is that long streak of foaming white, glittering down through the blackness of the night?

It is the curling white line of massy surge careering madly before the advancing storm, rolling up to crush the devoted ship in its weltering vortex.

"Port helm!" shouted the captain.

"Port it is."

Breathless silence reigned fore and aft.

Onwards rolls the curling bank of foam, quickening and quickening, and then with an awful crash, louder than the heaviest thunder roar, it bursts against the quivering hull of the hapless vessel.

"Hold on for your lives!"

Away flies the huge ship, tossing and rolling like a waif in a whirlpool, the thunderous monster billows pounding her shuddering sides, bashing at her stern, dashing down her breastworks and bulwarks, pouring over her smooth decks in a dense deluge, while every man of her half-drowned crew clings to masts, spars, belaying pins and lashings with the grip of grim death.

Scud, spray, and watery mist, leap up afar in shimmering clouds.

Again and again pour the dread, weltering seas over the decks, and sharp through the awful storm-roar rings a piercing yell of mortal horror and agony as three seamen are torn from their hold and swept away aft into the outer darkness.

Ahead—further and further ahead—careers the raging waters — white couriers of the tempest—and the deadliest peril is over !

Still the red, fighting lanterns gleamed like demon eyes in the inky darkness.

A light puff of cool air wafted over the parched decks.

Ablaze ! sky and sea glaring in a living blaze, each tiny wrinkle on the bulging swell, the far lone arc encircling the water-plains, the wild dark clouds, the reeling hull, the pencilled rigging, the gilded prow, all aglare !

Utter darkness !

Then an awful crash, and the prolonged, detonating thunder-roll rattling, growling, rumbling, dying far away.

Tomb-like darkness, death-like stillness !

The crew tumble up on to the deck.

Again the awful glare; leaping through the vault of bluish brightness, the fierce, forked lightnings flash.

A wild scream rings from hull to trucks.

The ship is struck by lightning !

A sulphurous smell pervades the vessel.

A white smoke curls up from the hatchways forward.

" Fire ! "

Jack rushes forward in the wake of the lieutenants, who beckon him.

He is the first to rush down the ladder.

He starts back with a cry of horror.

At his feet lies heaped the blackened corpse of one of his dearest messmates.

Our hero, Jack, exerted himself to the utmost, and, though severely scorched, worked like an English boy, as your Briton, whatever his faults may be, alone can work.

Palely glow the wild streaks on the far sky-line, the topmasts are burnished by the rising day-beams, and from the unburdened hearts of sixty gallant fellows rises an exultant huzza, proclaiming that the fire is extinguished, and the good barque " Titania " once more bears on her course in safety.

Jack Rushton accompanied the captain, the two lieutenants, and another midshipman below, to examine the state of the lower decks.

Crouched against one of the bulkheads, the negro, Pompey, was found; little Nellie sat on his knee, mute and trembling; a sash bound round her waist was tied to the negro's arm.

The child sprang forward to meet her father.

The captain embraced her with fatherly tenderness.

For the first time he displayed perceptible agitation.

" What does this mean, Master Pomp ?" he asked, lifting the silk sash.

"What dat ar mean, sar? Dat mean if 'pose de ole ship founder, me swim wid lilly missee so long um can; pr'aps find plank, den can get to de islands; 'pose not, dis child nebba leab young missee till he dead outright. Berry grad, sar, no want um; make um cumgratulation, sar."

"You're a faithful fellow."

"Iss, sar; ole Pomp de boy, sar."

CHAPTER III.

BOARDED BY PIRATES.

"Land ho! land on the lee bow!"

The cheering cry from aloft brought Jack and the other midshipmen on deck to the lee side.

The vessel now lay off a lovely palm-crowned island.

The captain's little daughter was gambolling with the negro on the quarter-deck, her silvery laughter mingling with his buffoonish but merry yah-yahing.

Suddenly the look-out uttered a startling cry—

"Sail, ho!"

A beautiful craft—a schooner, low, dark, and lateen-rigged — appeared gliding round a long range of rocks that ran out from one side of the island.

"By gum; dat a pirate!" gasped Pompey. The sudden change of expression in his black face from gay to grave was almost ludicrous.

The captain leaped on to the quarter, and instinctively clutched his child.

He stood for one moment transfixed with anguish and despair, cast one agonized glance upon the sweet, wondering face of his little daughter, then by a powerful effort resumed his duty.

"Mr. Hawser," said the captain, calmly addressing the boatswain, "tell the drummer to beat to quarters."

The order was obeyed with promptness, and at the first tap of the rattling air the men, who were clustered on deck or in the rigging, rushed to their various posts.

The armourer and his assistants now appeared on deck, carrying under their arms bundles of boarding pikes and naked, flashing cutlasses, which they distributed to the men.

The lieutenants, mids, and other officers, with pistols in their belts, and swords or dirks by their sides, took their station on the quarter.

It must be remembered that at the period of our story vessels in the East India Company's service were equipped for warfare in all respects like men-of-war.

All being in readiness the command was given—

"Silence for and aft!"

The captain sprang upon the main gangway.

He took off his hat.

His hair waved in the wind, and the roseate sunbeams burnished his pale, high brow.

"My boys," he cried, gallantly, "no mercy can be looked for from yon dingy devils; you know that. Your sole hope of deliverance rests in your own brave hands. You are Englishmen; English mettle has before to-day wrought wonders. At the worst, which is better—to die in hot action like brave men or be butchered in cold blood, or forced to walk the plank, by these Malay scums? Let me have your answer, and let me know by its sterling ring that it comes from the core of your stout hearts, in a sturdy cheer for England!"

"HURRAH!"

Once more the captain stood on the quarter-deck, and cast a steady glance in the direction of the pirate-schooner.

Three boats, two of them *proas*—canoes of a peculiar construction, which will hereafter be particularly described—the third a large row-boat pulling six oars, were seen gliding through the sparkling waves towards their prey.

The proas were manned with a motley crew of most villanous-looking ruffians of every shade of colour—Malays, Chinese, Japanese, Javans, Papuans, Pintadoes and Mestizoes—armed to the teeth with pikes, sabres, linstocks, creeses, bows and arrows, clubs, axes, yataghans, and other outlandish weapons.

The wretches in the row-boat, sun-swart as they were, appeared to be Europeans, probably Spaniards or Portuguese; a villain, taller and more tawdrily attired than his companions, sat in the stern sheets with a drawn scimitar in his hand.

The hideous black flag rippled up to the main-mast of the schooner.

The captain of the "Titania" kneeled down by the side of a long stern-chaser, from which the oiled canvas that protected it from the spray and heavy seas had been whipped off.

"Won't you hail the boats, sir?" asked the first mate, handing the speaking-trumpet by its lanyard.

"Aye, Mr. Dale," returned the captain, grimly, as he placed his hand on the trunnion of the carronade, "this is our mouth-piece."

In deep silence the officers watched the motions of the proas, which had forereached the row-boat, and came soaring swiftly down under press of their strange-shaped sails of cocoa-matting, the fiendish crews brandishing their flashing weapons, and yelling like hungry hyenas.

The captain once more stooped beside the long gun, and directing the men who served it by significant gestures and curt commands, pointed it himself.

Then he rose and glanced eagerly at the foremost proa, now scarce a cable's length astern.

"Steady, my men," he said. "Make ready! Fire!"

The match was instantly applied to the priming.

A thick cloud of white smoke bursts from the cannon's mouth—a sheet of living flame, and then a thunderous report shakes the vessel, while the heavy iron rips through the air, and smashes into the side of the large but frail canoe, cleaving her in twain, and strewing her *débris* on the face of the deep.

Her crew were seen bobbing like corks upon the foamy swell, while their comrades in the other boats howled their vengeance with all the fury of raging demons.

The crew of the "Titania" cheered.

"Well done!" cried our boy hero, who was standing beside the boatswain. "What think ye of that, Mr. Hawser?"

"Belay!" grunted the old tar. "We sailed on a Friday, and ne'er a one on us will trouble either the sail-maker or the quarter-master of graves!"

Meantime the schooner had once more got under weigh, and had crawled within gunshot of the "Titania," and rounded too under her lee-quarter.

Gone! the pirate-ship has vanished! In her place on the gloomy waters rests a dense, white thunder cloud, from whose bosom spurt red, blinding, lightning flashes, and with a dreadful roar, swift, massy bolts sweep fiercely, and come bashing into the fore-part of the doomed and already disabled brig.

One heavy shot passes right through the heart of the forestay, the jib-boom is shivered and carried away, the fore-topmast with all its gear topples and comes clattering down, and goes over the side.

Almost in the same instant the row-boat and the proa, with their gangs of sea-robbers, are rocking under the star-board-quarter.

"Away there, boarders!" shouted the captain, through his speaking trumpet. "Sweep the hell-hounds from the decks!"

But the grapnels had been thrown, the boats securely hooked on, and a motley crowd of fiendish desperadoes, whooping, yelling, taunting, cursing, cut away the nettings and scrambled on to the deck.

Their leader, a black-eyed, olive-hued villain, gaudily dressed and armed with a bright scimitar, rushed at the captain.

The two commanders furiously engaged.

All was uproar, madness, and horror; pistols crackled, hand-weapons clinked and slashed, sulphurous smoke enveloped all in chaos.

Jack was assailed by a hideous-looking Japanese, who thrust a clumsy pistol into his face. It snapped in the pan, and with a downright blow of his cutlass, Jack cleft the ruffian's smooth, shaven pate to the chine.

In the next moment the reeking sword was dashed from his hand by a pike wielded by a huge, black savage—a Papuan, of horrible countenance.

Jack seized the heavy gold ring pendent from the black ruffian's nose, and fiercely wrenching down his head, contrived, ofter a tough scuffle, to snatch the handspike from his grip.

The captain stumbled past, and reeling backwards, fell prone against tho bulwarks.

The pirate-chief, his black rolling eyes aglare, his long white teeth bright gleaming, hotly pursued, waving his blood-stained scimitar round his head.

Jack hurled off the shrieking savage and sped to the rescue of his noble captain; he smote down the pirate-captain with a blow of the lance.

Some of the merchant crew saw him fall, and uttered a fierce " hurrah !"

But the vengeful shout was premature, for just as their unfortunate captain rose on his knees, a bullet crushed into his temple, his face was instantly covered with blood, and he dropped into our hero's arms—stone dead !

The savage fight was kept up with the utmost desperation; the blasting of fire-arms, the clinking of hand-weapons, the quick trampling of feet waxed louder and louder; blood pooled on the deck and poured in crimson streams from the scuppers into the sea.

Our hero struggled through the *melée* to reach the main-hatchway, in some wild hope of saving the now orphaned child from the worst violence; he might even escape from a port with her and reach the island.

His foot is already on the companion stair. A heavy blow, suddenly dealt by an unseen hand, staggers him.

He reels—falls.

A blood-red mist—darkness — oblivion !

*   *   *   *   *

Consciousness slowly returning ; wild, hollow shouts—vague as the sea-roar in a shell—mingling, swaying, circling phantoms, as of a drunkard's dream.

Slowly and painfully poor Jack opens his quivering eyelids.

Where is he ?   A vast cavern, into which the broad, brilliant moon pours her flood of bluish, silver light, sparkling on the murderous weapons of a hundred ruthless desperadoes slumbering around him.

Alone in the Pirates' Lair !

Sick and giddy, Jack moves about on his hands and knees, checked by the jerk of a rope which binds him to the rocky wall.

What is this sharp object that he strikes his bare hand against ?

A flint !   He takes it up, and tremblingly crawls back under the shadow of the rock to which he is bound.

He sets to work, sawing at the strands of the rope with his sharp stone.

He has freed himself.

A yard or so from his position, the pirate-chief is sitting asleep, resting his head on a powder-cask, his arm bent over a huge pistol.

Jack creeps stealthily forward.

His fingers touch the pistol butt— the pirate emits a deep, fierce growl.

"BACK, YOU HOUNDS!" SHOUTED THE BOLD MID.

CHAPTER IV.

PLEASANT FOR JACK.

THE mid drew back with a tremor of mortal dread.

The pirate moved.

He drowsily passed the long, thin fingers of his left hand, glittering with jewelled rings, through his soft and glossy black curls; his right hand yet clutched a glass in which luscious tear-like beads of wine still clung.

This Jack did not observe as he crouched down in the dark shadow thrown by the barrel on the moonlit ground.

Once more his eye wandered fearfully round the vast cavern.

On all sides ruthless cut-throats of every colour, but all stained with the same deep dye of infamy, lay scattered, singly, or heaped in strange and motley groupings, in every posture of repose—above, along the ledges of protruding rocks, afar in the black recesses, close around in the pale blue glare of the vivid moonlight, weapons of all variety gleaming in their belts or in their grasping hands.

Curiously enough, in this moment of awful peril, Jack recalled to mind many a strange, wild legend he had read of spell-bound sleepers; of Holger Danske, who slumbers on his throne in the vaults of Cronenburgh, his red beard growing round the table on which his arm reclines; of Don Roderick, the Goth, and the British King Arthur, surrounded by their mailed, grim war-riors, all locked in an enchanted sleep that must endure till broken by some daring adventurer, who shall perform the rite that alone can dissolve the charm.

Breathing stillness—far more impressive than deathly silence—but hush!

Some one without the cave is softly chanting a low monotonous air.

It is the sentinel; a tall, lank Arab, who, with a long carbine on his shoulder, slowly paces before the arched entrance.

The Arab pauses, darkly stemming the full flood of the moonlight pouring in. There he stands—still as a statue, looking into the rocky vault.

Horror! As Jack cowers down, his cheek comes in contact with the sleeping pirate's foot! He must not stir—not a hair's-breadth—for dear life.

Again the sentry throws his carbine smartly to his shoulder, walks to the side of the yawning archway, and carelessly leaning his back against the rocks, fixes a vacant stare upon the moon-dazzled main.

On hands and knees, with cat-like caution, Jack creeps to the barrel.

He raises his hand—the tips of his fingers touch the cold brass boss at the end of the pistol butt.

He moves his hand round the stock, and gently, very gently, draws it from under the pressure of the unconscious pirate's arm, which sinks listlessly over the edge of the barrel.

He has the weapon in his hand.

What is to be done now?

He has not long to consider.

Still the same breathing silence pervades the pirate's lair.

CLASH!

The glass goblet has dropped from the pirate's clasp.

Gliding under the deepest shadows of the low-browed rocks, leaping over the moving bodies of the half-roused sleepers, Jack swiftly reaches his former position, quickly twists the rope about his waist, and stretches himself motionless. All this is conceived and executed in a moment.

The chief and at least a dozen other sleepers sprang to their feet, while the sentry rushed into the cave, his long carbine poised in his hands.

" Holà!" exclaimed the chief, rubbing his eyes and glaring upon the sentinel. " What noise was that, Azim?"

The question was asked in Spanish, and in the same tongue the Arab readily answered.

" It came not from without, Sahib, but from within—some one was moving here."

The pirates grasped their arms, and with a growl of Babylonian execration glanced round the cavern.

" Carrambo!" laughed the pirate, " the wine was strong, I must have fallen asleep with the cup in my hand; it has smashed, you see, and the sound awaked us —— But, che demonio!— where's my pistol?"

Jack, who had learned a little Spanish while abroad, perfectly understood all that was passing.

However, his start of surprise was natural enough when a deep, gruff voice replied in English,

" Here, cap'en, here it is."

Peeping cautiously through his half-closed lashes, our hero perceived a short, burly, broad-shouldered seaman kneeling, with the pistol in his huge fist.

" All's right," returned the pirate-chief, also speaking in English, though with a slight foreign accent. " Give it me, shipmate."

" Dat ar buccra boy—Mass' Ambrose; 'spec' he no dead," said a negro, turning his hideous face towards our luckless mid. " Hi! me cut him troat, sa, den no can make bobbery."

" Hold! bring a link," said the chief.

A pig-tailed Chinaman scampered off, and disappeared through a black arch, from which, in another moment, a red span of lurid light streamed athwart the cave, and the Chinaman re-entered with a flaming torch flaring in his sallow hand.

Poor Jack's situation was critical; but, with the cunning endurance of a fox shamming death, he stirred not a muscle, only venturing to peer through his lids at the galaxy of dreadful eyes fiercely glaring around him in the torch-light.

" Is he alive?" asked the chief.

The Englishman, thrusting the others aside, bent over the boy, and pulled down his lower jaw. Brave Jack did not flinch under this operation, and had the presence of mind not to re-close his mouth when his stern-looking countryman had relaxed his grip.

The seaman then opened the poor boy's eyelids, and peered into his quivering eye-balls.

" Is he dead?"

" I think so, cap'en."

" Place your hand over his heart."

" *I'm lost!*" thought Jack, who felt his frightened heart thumping almost audibly against his ribs.

He felt the seaman's rough hand thrust through his shirt, tearing out the buttons, then a heavy pressure on his warm, quick throbbing side.

——— No!

" *One friend! Thank God!*"

" Muy ben! Let him alone, comerado."

But, regardless of the captain's injunction, the negro drew a long, flashing knife, and touched the boy's neck with the fine, keen point of the blade.

" Better um make sure ob de young cuss."

" Avast, you black beast!" roared the English seaman, bestowing a heavy kick on the sable ruffian, that sent him staggering full a dozen yards. " Would you make the señor's bed-chamber a common shambles, you butcherly lubber?"

This sally provoked a general laugh, in which even the captain joined.

" A handsome boy," he muttered, with a chuckle. " He fought like the Cid Campeador. Pity he died; 'twould have been rare sport to have tested his mettle with the embers and red-hot pincers; but if he had quailed I should have killed him, so 'tis no matter."

" Don Pablo, shall I throw the body into the sea?" asked another ruffian— a Portuguese.

" Manana—it will do to-morrow; the night is young, and I am sleepy," returned the chief, yawning. " Ambrose, relieve the watch on the Palm Rock."

" Aye, senor," returned the Englishman, and, casting a furtive look at the apparently lifeless boy, he bit his lip, and rolled out of the cave, followed by five or six companions, making a tremendous clatter with their clumsy firelocks.

" Clear away, amigos, it is not wholesome to stand staring on the heretic brat," cried the chief, in a tone of impatience. " Let us to sleep again,— Sancho, set the link in yonder sconce by the wall of the inner cell. Leave it burning there, and bring me another cup of montillado."

Soon all was hushed.

The chief, after tossing off a glass of the wine, lighted his cigarito, and sat beside the cask, on which he reclined his arm, smoking and brooding grimly.

The moon had by this time travelled past the verge of the arched entrance of the cavern, and the place where the pirate-chief reclined was now enshrouded in deepest gloom; the red spark of the cigarito burnt brightly in the surrounding darkness.

Jack still lay in torture on the hard stones.

He dared not move.

At last the spark went out, and soon after our brave mid knew by the chief's deep breathings that he had once more sunk to sleep.

Jack pondered.

The relieved watch would probably soon return from the Palm Rock, of which he knew not the locality; it might be close at hand; at any rate, no time should be lost.

Some of the murderers around him might be yet awake; even so, it was pitch dark where he was lying, and the pirates had sheered off to a respectable distance from the " dead heretic."

The torch was burning in the inner cell, but no red ray penetrated into the principal vault; he would crawl through the rocky passage which led to the cell, he might find some outlet, and certainly it was as good " to die and go, as die and stay."

Bracing up his nerves for the perilous effort, he crept stealthily round the corner of the rock-way not far off, and followed its windings for a few yards, when, upon turning a sharp angle, he saw the torch blazing in a spacious recess, the floor of which was cumbered with sea-chests, sail-cloth, oars, nets, spars, and the like.

A pistol lay upon one of the lockers.

Jack eagerly caught it up, and, on examination, found it to be charged and primed.

He took the torch in one hand, and the pistol in the other; and thus guided and armed, made his way along the narrow passage, which wound onwards and past the cell.

The heat in the narrow tunnel became stifling, and through the sullen silence thrilled many a little piercing sound— a sudden, startling " buzz," or a shrill " tcick," as, attracted by the glare of the link, myriads of extraordinary insects crawled out from their retreats in the crevices and holes of the walls, or the floor of the rock-way, waving their horrid antennæ, trailing their long, many-feeted bodies, or whizzing their gauzy or metallic wings—mosquitoes wheeled; hideous, crawling centipedes made off to their hiding-places, while

here and there lobster-like scorpions ran rapidly, their venomous tails twined over their heads ready to turn either way for attack or defence; flies, gnats, and stingers innumerable powdered the air, while black ants specked, and bronze beetles studded, every part of the surface of the rocks.

Keeping off this plague of flies by waving his smoking torch about his head, our daring mid pushed on resolutely, till, stumbling down a rugged stair, he found himself in a wide and vaulted chamber of the cavern.

Looking about him, he was struck by the resemblance of the scene to that depicted in his old, well-thumbed volume, on the bed-room shelf at home, in dear England—the robbers' treasury in the " Forty Thieves."

Piled and stacked and lumbered on every side were valuables of every description—bales of silks and other stuffs, chests, casks and packages, bulkheads, money sacks, heaps of vessels of beamy gold and silver, gilded and damasked couches, delicate, richly carved and inlaid panels of fragrant cedar, and even fragile wares of glass and clear reflecting mirrors.

" Was it possible," reasoned Jack, " that that temple of Mammon was neither concealed nor even closed? He must be walking in a dream."

He paused, and turned a shuddering glance backwards at the steps and the entrance above him.

The unprotected state of the treasure-cave was fully accounted for; the entrance had been found inconveniently narrow, and the work of enlargement was going on; a heap of rocky fragments lay on one side of the porch, the massive old door leaned against the other.

But was there no dragon, no living guardian, to watch this treasure?

This query was instantaneously answered.

Flash, *crackle!* and a thousand reverberating echoes.

CHAPTER V.

GUNPOWDER PLOT.

In the same moment that the half-caste leaped up from his recumbent posture, Jack caught the quick, deadly gleam of his wild black eyes, and felt the menace.

He ducked; the bullet sped over his head and flattened against the hard opposing rocks.

Now, Jack, at him! but reserve your shot; that leaden pellet and pinch of powder in your barrel is worth more in your extremity than a nugget of pure gold and a bushel of gold-dust.

The better part of valour is discretion, but discretion does not always mean running away.

Jack was truly, calmly brave, and therefore he acted discreetly.

Leaping upon the tawny miscreant he dashed the flaming torch in his face, pinning him against the wall, and firing his crisp, curly hair; then, with a stunning blow of the pistol-butt, he stretched him on the earth.

One foot on the breast of his prostrate foe, panting, the cold, clammy sweat bedewing his forehead, Jack lingered and listened.

A hollow roar of echoing, distant voices poured down the passage by which he had come hither.

The report of the gun-shot had roused the pirates—he was pursued!

He rushed frantically about to find some outlet for escape.

Nearer, nearer, nearer, came the swift trampling footsteps.

An aperture, just large enough to admit the passage of his body, appeared at the far end of the cave.

Off Jack! the avengers are behind you.

Our fugitive was once more threading a maze, more narrow and intricate than the last, through clouds of dust and showers of insects.

He kept a miser's grip upon his torch and pistol, and, though his every limb quivered with mortal terror, he "screwed his heart to the sticking place," and fiercely determined to die rather than surrender.

Once more he was in a roomy hollow of the rocks.

A few spars, some rusting grapnels and ringbolts, a locker—but yonder!

A cask, from the bung-hole of which a train of black powder streaked the rocky floor!

Jack struck his foot against a stone.

He stumbled and fell.

The flame of the torch came in contact with the gunpowder train.

A phiz, and a bright, red flash.

Jack, in an instant, brushed away the powder with the palms of his hands.

He snatched up the half-extinguished torch, and, quivering in every nerve, his ears ringing, his heart throbbing desperately, he rose to his feet.

Still nearer, and swifter, and louder sounded the rush of many feet.

The poor middy glanced around him in a frenzy of rage and dread.

He found that the large and vaulted cavern looked out upon the sea.

It was oppressively hot, and the sky without pitch dark, the only light appearing in the outer gloom being the lantern that rocked at the prow of the pirate schooner anchored abreast the island, and its bright rippling reflection on the black water.

Suddenly the cavern was illumined by a dazing electric flash, and the sky, seen through the entrance of the cave, riven with zigzag streams of fierce lightning, the dark hull and pencilled rigging of the schooner standing forth in black, sharp relief against the blue flaring sea and sky.

Then the prolonged and awful thunder roll burst upon his ears.

Again all was dark, but for the lurid, smoky flare of the torch.

Yelling like a pack of ravenous jackals, a crowd of savage wretches in almost every variety of race and colour poured into the cave, and surrounded him.

Our hero at once set his foot upon the barrel, and, with one hand, lowering the flame of the torch to the hole of the powder cask, with the other pointed his pistol at the head of the foremost of his assailants, a gigantic negro—a Cori-mante—who advanced upon him, a creese or crooked dagger flashing in each hand.

"Back, you bloodthirsty hounds!" shouted the bold mid, in all the fiery energy of desperation. "If I must die I will yet avenge myself and my murdered shipmates. Approach one step, either of you, and I will fire the gunpowder and blow you all to atoms."

"Mashalla," roared Azim the Arab, pointing his carbine, "Cut the son of Shietan to pieces."

"Eigh; 'pose yo mad, young buccra!" laughed the negro, as he brandished the creese above his head. "Tink yo 'scape de senor? Yo no sabé! he Obeah man. Nebba nobody 'scape he; he burn yo eye out wid red hot pincer—yah! yo trow down de link and gib up dat pistol; yo hear, sa?"

"Never, you black villain!" shouted Jack. "Stand back, or here goes with a brace of bullets. I warn ye all that when I have counted twelve I will set light to the powder; and so sheer off, for every second is precious."

And still keeping the flame in dangerous nearness to the powder he shouted sternly—

"One—two—three——"

Flash! Bang!

The cavern rang with ear-splitting reverberations.

Azim had fired his carbine, and the bullet flew past our hero's cheek, and flattened against the opposite wall of rock.

Maddened with indignation, Jack

blazed away right into the middle of the crowd.

A yell, like the scream of a wounded baboon, proclaimed that the negro was hit.

The crowd swept backwards, seemingly cowed, and, for the moment, terror-stricken.

Jack dashed down the torch upon the barrel.

The next instant he saw the cask rolling swiftly across the cave as if propelled by a kick, and felt himself grasped behind in a grip of iron.

He tried in vain to release himself from that strong, tight clutch; he turned his head and beheld the dark, tanned face, the lank, raven black hair, and the deep-set, fierce black eyes of the terrible and sullen-looking English seaman who had saved his life.

The crowd of miscreants now returned to the charge with redoubled fury.

" Kill him !" shouted the Spaniards.

This cry for blood was re-echoed in a dozen outlandish dialects.

Linstocks, guns and pistols were presented, and steel weapons brandished at the captive.

Ambrose relinquished his hold of the boy, and placed himself before him.

" Stand clear, comeradoes," he growled, in a deep, bass voice, waving his hand; " I will manage this affair."

Poor Jack looked at him eagerly.

But no encouragement was to be read in that dark, sullen, scowling face.

Behind the Englishman stood a motley group of pirates, with carbines in their hands, evidently the sentries relieved from the Palm Rock.

" You are my countryman, sir," pleaded Jack to Ambrose. " I appeal to you; if you have one spark of manly feeling, protect me from these scoundrels."

" Avast !" growled the other, frowning darkly. " You have forfeited your life by your foolhardiness; I cannot save you."

" Kill me then, quickly," returned Jack; " I would rather die by your hand than be left to the mercy of these Malay tigers."

At this moment arose a general shout.

" Silence ! Don Pablo is coming."

Our hero started with a sickening qualm.

He turned hastily to behold the pirate-chief, who at the moment entered the cavern, accompanied by four or five companions, Spaniards and Portuguese.

Despite his abhorrence of the leading villain's hellish character, Jack could not help feeling a thrill of admiration at his eminently dashing and handsome appearance.

He was, in truth, a splendid-looking fellow; his every motion a study of native grace; his form of matchless symmetry; his face, though olive-hued, perfect in feature; his great, fierce black eyes shone with hauteur and sternness; his raven hair was long, black, and silky as a woman's; his teeth, a row of flashing pearls, shaded by a soft, black curling moustache; his air had all the stateliness of an hidalgo of the bluest blood; the only thing that detracted from his beauty was the gash on his forehead, ill-concealed by the rich, parti-coloured bandanna swathed across his brow.

He was showily dressed in a jacket of blue velvet, embroidered with gold; his rich silk sash bristled with inlaid and jewelled weapons of curious make, and his finely-moulded legs were encased in high boots of untanned leather.

He fixed a stern, quelling glance upon our hero, which the brave boy returned with a glare of scorn and hatred.

The villanous gang were eager in their appeals to the captain to butcher the young spy, as they called their defenceless captive.

Once more poor Jack cast an anxious glance at Ambrose.

But the seaman had turned his head away, and stood with folded arms moodily apart.

Don Pablo, as he was always styled—being very punctilious in matters of dignity—coolly drew a long silver-mounted pistol from his sash, carelessly examined the priming and cocked the trigger.

Then his arched black brows met in a dread frown, and his thin lip curled in a cruel leer.

"Are you prepared to die, young sir?" he asked in English.

"Are you prepared to kill me?" returned Jack, assuming a dauntless air, for he felt that boldness would serve him best when dealing with such a customer.

"Malraya!" laughed the pirate. "And pray, sir, what but my own will can prevent me?"

"If you are a brave man——But, pshaw! what are you but a bloody and cowardly pirate!" returned our hero, with genuine fierceness—for he was enraged by the recollection of the ruthless slaughter of his kind captain and hearty messmates—getting reckless of his life, and, with true British pluck, revolted with self-scorn at the thought of craving mercy at the hands of the merciless, dastardly miscreant before him.

All started.

An exclamation of rage hissed through the pirate's white clenched teeth, and a pink flush suffused his olive cheek.

He grasped the pistol viciously.

"Have a care," he growled, "I am not used to brook insolence; untimely death is never an easy doom, but it has its extremes of bitterness. Do you know, sir, that for a slighter offence than this impertinence, I have punished my adversaries by wringing out life in refined and protracted torments? I hate all men but my own followers; I detest your proud and overbearing nation beyond all others. I shall kill you, but it is through your own fault if your sufferings are needlessly prolonged."

"Incarnate devil, I defy you!" shouted Jack, at the same time bursting into passionate tears. "Kill me as you killed my shipmates; I can die as bravely as they."

"And yet you weep," sneered the pirate.

"Not for myself," returned poor Jack, dashing the drops from his eyes. "But why do I palaver with this cutthroat villain," he exclaimed suddenly, "when I have the pistol still in my grasp?"

He levelled the weapon at the pirate's head.

He fired.

But Ambrose struck up his arm, and the bullet thudded against the rocky roof of the cavern.

A score of pistols, linstocks and carbines were levelled at the head of the reckless lad.

Ambrose threw himself before the boy.

"A brave slip, senor; pity to kill him," said the Englishman, with a smile.

He spoke in Spanish.

"Jesu Maria!" cried the "Don," crossing himself devoutly, "'Twas a narrow escape for me; fire on the Yenglesa whelp."

"Hold!" thundered Ambrose, "let me first have a word with the senor."

So saying, he took the chieftain apart, and conversed with him in a low, eager whisper.

With fainting heart, Jack watched the scowling faces of the two pirates.

At length Don Pablo and the Englishman advanced towards him.

"I will grant you a reprieve," said the Spaniard, with a grim smile, "but you must consider yourself my slave. I shall appoint you my personal attendant, and your life, which I have spared from a motive of caprice, I may take at any moment if you offend me; remember, that you exist only upon my sufferance."

Jack's cheek flushed hotly; he was about to make an angry reply.

Ambrose, however, quelled him by a stern glance.

"Thank him!" murmured the Englishman in his ear. "Say 'gracias, senor.'"

But Jack kept grim silence.

The pirate watched him closely.

Then he burst into a long loud laugh.

"Away with him!" he cried. "I leave him in your charge, Ambrose, and shall hold you responsible for his safe keeping. Malraya, he's one of the true British bull-dog breed; I wish I had a hundred such followers!"

CHAPTER VI.

WHY MARK AMBROSE TURNED PIRATE.

JACK RUSHTON was conducted by the English pirate into a large vault-like chamber in the rocks.

Ambrose had dismissed his companions, and taking the link in his hand, had moodily and silently preceded our hero.

Jack looked around him with a look of curiosity and interest.

The place presented a peculiar aspect On one side there was a niche in the wall, occupied by a figure of the Madonna, rudely carved in stone, and on all sides were many strange inscriptions cut in the living rock.

A hammock was slung across the chamber, and the place was furnished with a beautifully inlaid table, evidently the spoil from some plundered vessel; a log of wood and one empty cask served for seats.

The cavern was lighted by a flaring oil lamp, depending by a chain from the roof, and throwing its lurid, fitful light on trophies of sheeny steel weapons and finely-mounted fire-arms, arranged around the walls with much tastefulness.

A gilded couch stood in a corner, to which Ambrose pointed.

"You are weary, my boy,"· said he, in a voice gruff but kindly; "rest yourself."

Our hero, who was exhausted with pain and excitement, made no other answer than by a grateful smile, and stretched his weary limbs upon the soft cushioned sofa.

Ambrose trimmed the lamp, drew his pistols from his belt, took off his sword from his side, and hung the weapons on a nail in the wall.

Then he retired into a little cell at the far end of the vault, and after awhile returned with a bottle of wine, some biscuits, and a piece of roasted meat, which he spread out upon a table, upon which he had previously set a couple of richly-chased silver goblets.

"Come, lad," he said, with a faint smile, "since I am to be your gaoler, whatever happens you shall not starve while in my keeping."

The exciting events of the day had not spoiled Jack's appetite.

He rose, and murmuring his thanks, seated himself at the table.

"Shake hands, little messmate," said the pirate, extending his hard palm.

Our hero turned pale, and recoiled, shuddering.

The pirate frowned.

He got up from the barrel, and moodily paced through the cavern.

"Why don't you eat?" he said, after a pause, folding his arms, and casting a peculiar look upon his prisoner.

"I will. I thank you with all my heart for your kindness," returned Jack, in a quivering tone.

He made an attack upon the viands before him, and partook moderately of the wine, which he found to be of a rare good quality.

The pirate seated himself on the couch, and watched the boy with strange interest.

Still the thunder growled without, and the waves kept up their fierce and hollow roar.

From time to time Jack cast a furtive glance at the pirate, who seemed lost in deep thought.

At length, having finished his supper, Jack removed the log of wood which served for a seat, to some distance from the table, and looked inquiringly at the pirate.

The man remained silent, his arms tightly folded across his broad breast, and his eyes fixed sullenly on the ground.

At length he started up, and, drawing a deep sigh, advanced to the boy, and once more held out his hand.

"Shake hands," he said.

"Do not think me ungrateful," said Jack, lowering his glance, "but, indeed, I would rather not."

"And why?"

"Because — be-cause," stammered Jack, "your hand is stained with the blood of my poor shipmates."

A Portrait of DON PABLO, Gratis with this Number.

"HE TOOK UP A LARGE SABRE AND POINTED TO A DENT IN ITS EDGE."

"As you please," returned the pirate, with a sickly smile; "my hands are not clean, I know."

He passed his brown fingers through his raven black hair, and, as if stung by remorse and passion, clenching his teeth, he hissed forth some unintelligible mutterings.

Jack looked at him with awe.

His dark eyes were fixed on vacancy, and his face worked with ill-suppressed emotion.

"I fear you will consider me thankless," said Jack, softly; "but I assure you that I feel very, very grateful for the protection you have afforded me. The life you have saved is yours; I would gladly lay it down to serve you. But my mother has taught me," and here poor Jack's voice grew faint, and the tears sprang to his bright blue eyes, "that I should not shake hands with those whom I cannot esteem. She wished me to be sincere in my dealings with everybody, and so I tell you frankly that, though I would do anything in my power in return for your kindness to myself, I cannot forget your treatment of my poor captain and messmates."

Jack paused, as if aghast at the bold impulse which had prompted him to make this rash speech.

The pirate stared at the boy.

He grimly smiled.

"You may say what you like, you will not offend me."

"I—I trust not," rejoined Jack, with genuine fervour. "I hope my motive is not misunderstood."

"No," sighed the pirate; "there was a time when I should have refused to have taken a hand stained with blood.

Blood! pah! I have come to look on the shedding of blood with as much indifference as the pouring out of water. Custom reconciles one to anything."

"How terrible!" gasped Jack; "but yet you saved my life——"

"And tried to save the lives of your shipmates."

"Is that true?"

"True! Lying is a coward's vice, and, at least, I am not a coward," returned the pirate, gloomily. "Harkye, little cherry, I was not of the boarding party; I knew by her bunting that your vessel was English, and I tried to dissuade the senor from attacking her; but all in vain. So come, your honest hand will not be polluted by grasping my guilty one. I have never injured you: I will use all my influence to protect you from harm. Come, will you shake hands now?"

"Yes," said Jack, getting up.

The pirate took hold of both his hands, and gripped them strongly, fixing a steady look upon the boy's frank face.

"So, that's hearty," he said, in a tone of pleasure; "you are a fine lad. You spoke of your mother?"

"God for ever bless her!" cried Jack, unable to repress his tears. ██ how I rejoice when I think that she does not know of my situation; she would kill herself with grief."

"And is your father living?"

"No; my mother is a widow; I am her only child."

"Poor soul," rejoined the pirate. "It is well, as you say, that she does not know what has befallen you; the senor would contaminate a saint; if he takes a fancy to you, he will scoff away all your good principles, and in a month you will become as bad as the rest."

"Never!" returned Jack, vehemently.

"And what is your name?"

"Jack Rushton."

"And mine is Mark Ambrose; and so we know each other, and are friends."

There was a pause.

"Talk," said Ambrose, simply, at length breaking the silence. "I like to hear you talk; your English accent is music in my ears, for, though the senor, the negro Matanza, and several others of the band, speak our language, they talk as foreigners. I have not heard the voice of an Englishman for two years."

"Then you have not boarded an English ship lately?"

"No; there is a compact between me and the senor, by virtue of which I am excused from waging war with my own countrymen, unless in defence of the band. But tell me, lad, what port do you hail from?"

"From Plymouth, where I was born," answered our hero.

A dark shade overcast the pirate's face.

He appeared to be greatly moved by this simple reply.

"From Plymouth!" he gasped. "Did you ever hear of Sir Richard Varney of that town?"

"Oh, yes; the captain of the ' Fearless,' poor Captain Transom, knew him well; when we lay off the old place, he came aboard with his lady."

"Ha! and you saw her then?" asked the pirate, quickly.

"A very beautiful lady," rejoined our hero, "though she looks sad and timid, and seems to be much afraid of that surly old commodore, Sir Richard. Oh, I remember her well; I was in the captain's gig when she was put ashore from our ship. I have heard that her father was but a poor man, a channel pilot; but, to judge by her appearance, one would take her to be a lady born, her manners are so refined, so gentle."

"Avast!" growled the pirate, "do not praise her. The curse of my heart cleave to her and blight her! She was my ruin!"

"Lady Varney!"

"Marion Leigh; and she is still beautiful, eh?"

"The loveliest lady that ever I beheld," rejoined our hero, warmly.

"Lovely!" hissed the seaman through his gnashing teeth; "aye, the sea is ' lovely ' when it slumbers in fair weather, and sparkles in the sunlight, but there's treachery in its smile; these tropic isles are ' lovely,' but they are nests for the serpent and the scorpion, and lairs for the fierce pirate. Ah, boy, you are young, your heart is free; you know nothing of those storms of the soul, the passions! Lovely! aye—false—false!"

Ambrose hid his face in his hands, and groaned bitterly.

Then, as if unable to bear his agonising thoughts, he leaped up. Backwards and forwards he paced, his head bent on his breast and his arms folded.

Jack gazed at him wonderingly.

He stopped in his walk, laughed harshly, and again nervously passed his fingers through his crisp, black locks.

"Lovely!" he muttered. "Aye, she *was* lovely—there was the curse!"

"I suppose she was your sweetheart?" said Jack, bluntly.

The pirate made no answer.

He kept his measured pace, tramping through the cavern chamber with folded arms and downcast eyes.

Suddenly he walked to our hero's side, who was now seated on the couch, and clutched his arm.

"Harkye, lad! but no—you are tired —some other time."

"You are going to tell me why you turned pirate," cried Jack, with animation.

"It will ease my heart," said the pirate; "but I will not tell you now; it is almost daybreak; you require sleep."

"Aye; but I can't sleep till I have heard your story," returned Jack, with a boyish smile.

"Well, then, I will twist the yarn, and you shall judge whether I deserve pity or not. Yet, how can I excuse myself? I am a vile pirate, and those whom I destroy never wronged me; while *he*—*he* escapes. Oh! shall I never know the joy of wreaking my vengeance on him? Some day I will go to England and seek him out. I will not die till I have had my revenge!"

"'Vengeance is mine!' the Creator has said," returned Jack, seriously; "besides, we live but a little while, and there is justice hereafter."

"Your mother taught you that," sneered the pirate. "She is a woman, and women are less vindictive than men. If she had suffered the same kind of wrong that I have, she would

not preach patience, I'll be sworn. I open my heart to you, boy, I know not why; perhaps because you come from my native place, because you are frank, and bold, and loveable; however, you shall hear my story."

Again the pirate rose, and tramped about the chamber, speaking rapidly.

"I must begin at the beginning, then. I was born to the sea; my father was the master of a coasting vessel; my mother, too, came of a seafaring family. At sixteen I entered on the books of the 'Martha,' a merchant barque, bound for the river Plate, or, as I should say now, since I have had so much commerce with Spaniards, the Rio de la Plata; that was my first voyage. When I returned I was nearly nineteen. But I should have told you that the father of Marion Leigh rented a cottage adjoining my father's—they had been shipmates together—and that I and Marion were playmates from childhood."

The pirate paused, and an expression of fond and poignant regret passed over his face.

"Old Alan Leigh was poor; he had been damaged by the fall of some block or spar, which struck upon his head, and injured his brain, for often his wits were quite unsettled, and at all times he was a poor, shambling, helpless, grumbling creature.

"When I returned from sea, I asked for Marion, and found that that she had removed to a neighbouring village, having been adopted by a kind old vicar, who had sent her to school, from which she had but lately returned a fine lady.

"I did not half relish this news, especially as I was told by the neighbour folk that old Leigh had sworn that his daughter should marry none but a gentleman, and, with mad cunning, set up a story that he himself was descended from a good family; and the crazy old man would often point to a chest, in which he pretended were locked up deeds and papers to prove this assertion.

"However, I went to see my lass.

"It was then that I first knew how much I loved her; she was a being so bright and beautiful, that the passion she inspired in my wild heart was not a feeling of common affection and respect, but the blind adoration of a devotee for his idol.

"Ah, God! how I loved her!"

Ambrose turned aside his head.

Our hero could not see his face, but could tell by the heaving of his breast and the twitching of his fingers what a tempest was raging in the strong man's heart.

"Avast! 'tis the old story. You will weary of it."

"No," replied Jack; "I am much interested; pray go on."

"She drove me mad!

"She was so kind and gentle, but as cold and impassable as an iceberg.

"I acted like a fool and a brute, and in the frenzy of my despair, reviled her.

"She did not return me one evil word, but listened meekly to my wild upbraidings; but her father had wrung from her a promise to reject me.

"I extorted from her a half promise not to marry till my return from sea,

for I was about to sail in a ship outward bound for the Bermudas.

"I had entered for a term of two years.

"I tore myself away from her."

"And did she break her vows?" asked Jack.

"You shall hear. I had a prosperous voyage, made a good haul of rhino, had been promoted to the rank of second mate, and was homeward-bound.

"In the mid Atlantic our brig was overhauled by an infernal man-o'-war cutter; the lieutenant in command picked out the best hands of our crew, myself among them, and pressed us into the king's service."

"What a shame!" cried Jack, indignantly.

"Aye, mate; imagine my feelings when the 'Wyvern,' the name of the man-of-war on which I was a slave and a prisoner, lay off my own town, within sight of the very cottage where my beloved one dwelt, and I forced to keep my weary watch, and do my irksome duty, while almost frantic with disappointment and impatience, and thinking every moment that I must fling myself over the bulwarks, and risk my life to get to land."

"What, wouldn't they let you go ashore?"

"Not the pressed men; we were detained for fear we might desert."

"And did you see your sweetheart no more?"

"Listen. After we had lain at anchor for some days, orders were given to man the side to receive the captain; salutes were fired, and the flags run up. He came aboard, and proved to be a sour, severe-looking old ruffian ; in fact, Sir Richard Varney."

" And did he come alone ?"

" No ; he brought his bride with him," gasped the excited pirate. " I happened to be stationed at the gangway, and offered my hand to help her over the side ; she touched me ; I turned. Oh, that I had fallen dead at her feet ! It was she—my loved, loved Marion !"

" And did she recognise you ?"

" Why, lad, I had her in my grip," returned the pirate, with the touching simplicity of deep grief, his face working with agonising passion. " She shrieked and fainted in my arms ; and there stood I, clasping her in my tight embrace, and glaring my hatred upon the hoary old dotard who called himself her husband."

" I think she must have loved you, Ambrose, after all," said Jack, with a sigh.

" Well, there is one thing, though, that I must say for her. The first mate of the merchantman from which I had been pressed—a mean, sneakish hound, who always bore a grudge against me for being an abler seaman and a man more liked than himself—either from spite, or bribed by the titled villain who robbed me of my love, spread a report that I had died on the voyage."

" The scoundrel !"

" Marion was torn from my clasp, and borne below ; I was instantly seized, the quarter-master was sent for, I was put into irons, and confined in the hold. Days passed ; how, I know not, for time stood still with me. The ship sailed, and I was tried by my officers for insolence and insubordination."

" And was Sir Richard your judge ?"

" Aye, mate ; and it was from his lips I received my sentence."

" What villany and injustice !"

" I was lashed to the gratings, and my back torn by the bo'swain's cat ; but they might as well have lashed the mainmast as my insensible body ; my brain was in flames, my heart rent by harpies ; I was insensible to mere bodily suffering."

" I suppose you had a hard time of it under your jealous captain ?"

" I was stung to death with gnat stings," hissed the pirate. " Do what they would, they could find no fault with my seamanship or my performance of duty ; but they brow-beat, baited, and badgered me till one night I got out of my hammock and stole to the magazine, and should have fired it, and blown the ship off the face of the waters, but on my way I met one of the ship's boys reading a letter from his mother, and then my heart failed me."

" But how did you escape ?"

" For months I brooded over my wrongs ; time brought no alleviation to my grief and rage. I was again flogged for not saluting the captain as he passed me, and then recked of nothing but how to compass my revenge.

" One day, as the captain stood bullying a poor, trembling lad in the gun room, the devil was roused in my heart ; I lost all presence of mind, all care for my own life ; I seized a marlinspike, and, rushing upon the tyrant, stretched him senseless at my feet.

" Ah ! the delirious joy of that moment. I stamped my foot upon the prostrate tyrant, and yelled my defiance at the officers, who stood round, calling upon them to hack me to pieces; and I doubt not they would have taken me at my word, and have gashed me to death with their drawn dirks, but for the first lieutenant, who interposed to save me; but I had not killed the villanous captain—my revenge remains to be completed."

"Of course you were again arrested?"

"Aye, mate; and for weeks I gnawed my chains in the dark hold, two sentries keeping watch over me with loaded fire-locks."

"And with the prospect of death before you," rejoined our hero; "for, of course, had you been brought to trial, you must have been sentenced and swung off at the yard-arm."

"There was my comfort. All that life had of peace or pleasure was lost for me. Ah! how I wish I had submitted to my fall, and had escaped what followed. A mutinous spirit had broken out amongst the pressed men, and they looked upon my conduct rather with pity and approval than with abhorrence; and it was whispered in the forecastle that the only thing I deserved hanging for was the not striking hard enough.

"One of the sentries was a young fellow to whom I had done some service —what it was I forget now—but for which he was very grateful. He connived at my escape; a messmate brought me a file, with the aid of which I got free from my shackles. At dark I crawled out of the hold, and getting out through a port in the orlop deck, I dropped into the sea and escaped to this island, abreast of which the king's ship was anchored.

"For days I lay hid in the woods, narrowly escaping the boat's crew sent in pursuit of me.

"About a month elapsed, and more than once boats from passing vessels put in shore for water and provisions; but I was afraid to reveal myself to any of them, for fear they should discover the real state of my case, and give me up to a man-of-war.

"At length a schooner appeared off the coast, and a motley crew of fellows landed. They were pirates under the command of our present captain, Don Pablo Parades.

"I told my story to the Spanish skipper, showed him my fetter marks, and the weals and scars on my shoulders. He offered me a command on board his vessel, of which I have now the honour to be first-lieutenant."

"An honour, indeed!" cried Jack, contemptuously.

Ambrose smiled faintly.

"Belay," he said, rising, "I am not sorry that I have told you my story—a weight seems lifted from my heart; but it is time you went to rest. I shall turn in for a few hours only, but you can sleep as long as you please, or until the senor sends for you. I will take care that you shall not be needlessly disturbed."

Jack Rushton expressed his thanks in a tone of exhaustion, for he was terribly shaken by the wild events of the day, and felt faint and dizzy.

He threw off his jacket and shoes.

Ambrose arranged the couch for Jack to sleep upon, piling it with rich velvet cushions, and when our hero had stretched his stiffened limbs upon the downy bed, drew a gauze curtain over him to screen him from the stings of the mosquitoes.

He then got into his hammock.

The lamp was left burning.

Weary as he was, Jack felt too much excited for sleep.

A whirl of strange recollections confused his brain; it seemed that he had lived a century since he first found himself alone in the Pirates' Lair.

The incidents in the story, which he had listened to with such interest, seemed presented before his eyes with painful vividness, and he was for some time wide awake listening to the beating of the waves as they rushed up the beach and washed into the echoing caves along the coast, and to the fitful growling of the distant thunder.

At last he slept.

But his slumbers were broken by hideous visions. Again he was struggling in the fiery fight,—then hunted by the yelling Malay savages,—was then bound to the rocks, the cruel, satanic face of the pirate chief glaring over him, and the red-hot irons being thrust into his scorching eye-balls! He uttered a loud cry and started up.

"What cheer, lad?" cried Ambrose, springing from his hammock. "What ails ye,—what has frightened ye?"

"Oh! — nothing—" moaned poor Jack. "A dream—a horrible dream!"

CHAPTER VII.

DON PABLO PARADES, THE PIRATE CHIEF.

"Hi! yho! now dar, you young buccra cuss, why fo' you not turn out when yo hear um call—yha?" cried a harsh voice, arousing Jack from a refreshing doze into which he had at length fallen.

He started up from the couch, and stared, half-asleep half-awake, at the ugly black head of the Coromante, which peered through the sail-cloth curtain that screened the entrance of the cave.

"Ha! you wake now; dat better so for yo,' I tink, yong massa; if not wake, I gib yo' a bit o' my 'skeeter sting—dat make yo' open yo' darned heavy eye."

And the black savage shook his gleaming poignard.

"What do you want?" asked Jack, coolly.

"De senor hab send fo' yo'."

"All right, darkie; tell him I'll come," returned Jack, smiling, as he slipped on his shoes and deliberately tied the strings.

The negro spluttered with wrath.

"What dat yo' say, sa?" he roared. "Tell I come! Ye's better tell dat to de senor yo'se'f, yo' imp'rant dog."

"Don't flurry yourself," said Jack, walking across the room and pouring some water from a ewer into a basin and sluicing his face; "I shall be ready in a twinkling."

The negro seemed struck aghast at the boy's calmness.

"Yo' not lib long, dat I see,—yha—yha!" he sneered, curling up his thick lips till his face looked all mouth and fangs.

Jack did not deign to make any reply.

He threw on his jacket, parted his fair curls off his brow, and then said shortly,—

"Lead the way! I'll follow."

The Corimante gave a snort of disgust, and with an air of burlesque majesty swaggered out of the cell.

They emerged by a tunnel through the rocks at an opening in the cliff that walled one side of the island.

Not a little to Jack's surprise, the sun blazed at the meridian, and he was half blinded by its noontide blaze.

Becoming accustomed to the glare, however, he tripped lightly after the negro.

The island was a very fairy land of tropic luxuriance.

The woods rang with the screaming of parroquets, the chattering of monkeys, the croaking of tree frogs, and the loud, continuous, drowsy buzzing of the myriad insects.

Jack felt refreshed and inspirited by the beauty and brightness of the morning, and though his heart throbbed wildly, his step was bold and free, and his air as dauntless as ever.

After proceeding a few paces, Jack and his guide came upon a large group of pirates basking at the mouth of a high cavern.

Some lay stretched asleep, their faces shaded by their great straw hats from the sun's rays; others sat, listlessly smoking, upon the sides of the rocks; while, in several places, knots of picturesque vagabonds of various races were engaged in gaming, with as much zest and excitement as if their own life was the stake for which they played.

Many turned a lazy glance at the boy as he passed; but none spoke to him.

Jack looked about for Ambrose.

His friend was nowhere to be seen.

Entering the cave, however, he recognised him.

He stood leaning, with his usual melancholy air, against the rocky wall.

They exchanged one brief but significant look, and then once more the Englishman bent his eyes upon the earth.

But the personage who attracted his marked attention was the pirate chief himself, who rose as he entered, and made a most graceful bow.

He was very splendidly dressed, and his aspect was very romantic and dashing.

"Good morning, amigo," he said, in English, taking his cigaret from his lip, and waving his hand with a courtly air. "And how did you sleep last night?"

"Not very well, senor," returned Jack, boldly; "but better than I could have expected, under all circumstances."

The pirate laughed.

"You must not break your rest by dreaming of escape," said the pirate, with a treacherous smile. "And remember, it is dangerous to talk in your sleep. There was one ungrateful wretch whom I spared, and who lived amongst us long enough to learn how to cut throats without squeamishness; he raved in his sleep about hoisting signals to ships in the offing, and, whenever he could slink away unobserved, would prowl about the cliffs, and keep a look out to seaward. As he was so fond of watching, I gave him a permanent post as a sentinel of sea and land. Ha! ha! Senor Juan (so I shall call you for Jack)—English Jack —is a name I hate."

"And *fear*, my fine senor," thought our hero.

"But, harkye, young comrade—do you see that little black speck yonder?"

"Something dark and round on the top of that hommock of sand and shingles?"

"Aye; go and see what it is, and then return to me."

Jack stared with surprise.

However, at a look from Ambrose he turned to go.

"Very good, senor," said our gallant Jack. "But, whatever it is, I'll warrant I won't let it frighten me."

Our hero marched off to the mound of sand.

Upon reaching the top of it, he started back with a cry of dismay at the dreadful spectacle which presented itself.

The black speck which the pirate chief had sent our hero to look at proved to be—the head of a dead man!

The poor wretch to whom the pirate had alluded had evidently been buried quick in the earth as far as to the neck, with his face turned towards the sea, and left to starve to death.

But there was an expression of horror stamped upon the thin, withered lips, and the gaunt, famine-blighted cheeks, that caused our hero to draw back with a yell of dismay.

"Merciful heaven!" he exclaimed, clasping his hands and uplifting his eyes. "Can it be possible that the fiends who did this were really human?"

He turned and fled from the spot.

Perhaps it is necessary to inform our readers that the atrocities ascribed to the pirates are derived from fact, and that our purpose in giving a truthful picture of the lives and habits of such desperate villains is to disabuse the young mind of the false notion that there ever was or ever can be those chivalrous characteristics about robbers, pirates, and other like pests of society, which have been falsely portrayed in so many pernicious romances of crime.

When our noble Jack returned to the pirate chief, he advanced with a proud step, clenched teeth, and a frown on his manly brow.

"Well, Juan, what think you of the watch we keep; our sentry is true to his post, ha?" said the pirate.

"This piece of work is worthy of you, senor," gasped Jack, his brave eyes flashing a Briton's scorn.

"You flatter me," sneered the pirate, re-seating himself upon the cask; "but bring me a light for my cigaret."

Jack complied.

"Thanks; and now sit down by my side, and before taking my siesta for the afternoon, I will entertain you by a recital of some of the chief events of my life."

Jack obeyed, and listened to the horrible tale of murder and treachery with a feeling of wonder and disgust.

The pirate, in recounting his experiences, said that his name was Don Pablo Parades de Alcala; that he was descended from a very noble family, and at the death of his father had inherited vast possessions, but that he had lost all at the gaming tables, had killed a rival in love, and had involved himself in treasonous plots; and that, finding his own land too hot for him, he had raised a sum of money by means of forgery, and had expended it in fitting out a vessel, in which he intended trying his fortunes as a buccaneer.

Then he proceeded in the coolest and most triumphant manner to relate his various deeds of atrocities during his career as a pirate.

A pile of arms lay beside him.

In describing the slaughter of an English crew, he took up a large sabre, and pointed to a dent in its edge, caused, as he said, by its coming in contact with the head of the captain, a white-haired old man, who fought like a lion.

Just at this point the narrative was interrupted by a sudden outburst of quarrel between some Spanish and Portuguese ruffians disputing about the dice.

There was a terrible row and scuffle.

The Spaniards mingled together, cursing, foaming with rage, and gesticulating like maniacs.

It was in vain that the leader thundered his commands for silence.

Suddenly the shout arose—

"Gomez is stabbed!"

A man staggered across the cavern, and dropped like a stone, the blood gushing from his side.

In an instant the assassin was seized.

"Who has done this?" thundered Don Pablo.

"Pedro, senor; see, the knife is in his hand!" shouted a dozen voices.

"Enough. I will stop these brawls by a stern example," said the leader, with a dreadful scowl.

"Mercy!" shrieked Pedro, cringing down at the chief's feet, and embracing his knees. "Pardon, gracious senor; mercy!"

"Fra Valdez," said the pirate chief, turning to a villanous-looking desperado, dressed in the cassock of a priest, "the crucifix! Shrive this fellow; he has not a moment to live."

The chief devoutly crossed himself.

The Spaniards of his gang, in deep silence, sank on their knees; and, taking off their hats, piously prayed for the condemned.

"Mercy!" shrieked the grovelling wretch.

"It is too late," said the pirate chief, coldly; "but Fra Valdez shall say masses for the repose of your spirit. This act is needful for our common safety."

So saying, the miscreant drew a pistol, and, clapping it to the head of the shrieking Spaniard, deliberately blew out his brains.

"Remove the bodies," said the villain, calmly, as he replaced his still smoking pistol in his belt. "You see, Master Juan, I am not one to be trifled with. Another light for my cigaret—and now let us resume our story."

THE NEGRO SWAYED THE OAR ROUND HIS HEAD.

CHAPTER VIII.

JACK DEFIES THE TEMPTER.

For upwards of an hour the pirate chief continued, in a careless tone, to narrate his detestable adventures.

Jack Rushton sat listening, with an icy chill running through his blood, and a sickening qualm rising in his throat; he kept his eyes glued upon the pirate's handsome but satanic countenance with a gaze as of a bird fascinated by the eyes of a rattlesnake.

It is quite unnecessary to detail any of the horrible deeds which the cruel, treacherous, and ferocious villain narrated with a chuckle of pride and exultation.

"And so much for your dashing pirates!" thought Jack; "it is such wretches as these that have been sometimes painted as gallant, chivalrous follows—the most murderous and dastardly of thieves and cut-throats! I should like those who suppose that there can be anything generous or heroic in vile robbers and corsairs, to spend just one hour alone in the pirates' lair."

The pirate suddenly paused.

"Of what are you thinking, Juan, eh?" he asked, with a mellow laugh, as he gracefully reclined himself against the rock, shook the silky black ringlets from his sun swart forehead, and lazily puffed the smoke through his snow-white teeth.

Jack kept his eyes steadily fixed on the ground, blushed, but made no answer.

"Why don't you speak?"

"Thought is free, senor," returned our bonnie Jack, in a frank but serious tone; "we cannot help our thoughts. If I told you what was passing in my mind, you would be offended; and I do not wish to tell you a lie."

The pirate frowned darkly, and glared at the boy.

Jack turned deathly cold; his senses seemed numbed, the colour stole from his fresh, young cheek, and throbbed through his frighted heart; but with that noble courage of the true British boy, who feels fear but quells it by an effort of self-control, the upright youth fixed an unblenching look on the glowing, tigerish eyes of the Spanish miscreant.

The pirate, with a gesture of impatience, tossed aside his cigarette, half rose from his indolent position, and—perhaps unconsciously—laid his hand upon the jewelled hilt of a poignard, stuck through his sash of crimson silk.

"Mark me, Senor Juan," he said, contemptuously; "courage is one thing, insolence another."

"Indeed, senor, I did not mean to be insolent," was our hero's calm reply; "but I dare not tell you my thought."

"You dared not, eh?" laughed the pirate. "So, then, you dare not all things, my British lion-cub!"

"I am no braggart, I trust, senor," replied Jack, simply. "As my life depends upon your favour, I should be very sorry to offend you."

"I commend your prudence," sneered the pirate; "but you come of a nation of unmannerly boors; you English pique yourselves on what you call your bluntness, which is nothing but a dogged obstinacy that blinds itself to reason. Listen to me, Juan; you are a brave, fine lad, and I should be sorry if you provoked me to do you an injury."

"I thank you for saying that, senor. I am not insensible to your favour in sparing my life," returned Jack, with a gasp, glad of an opportunity of conciliating the ruffian without any sacrifice to his own good principles.

"Well, then," continued Don Pablo, "listen, boy; at your age the heart should be inspired with lofty aspirations—callous caution, that comes with advancing years, should be absent from bold and daring youth; this life is a life of warfare—this world is one great battle-field, where the strong must ever win dominion over the weak. Is it not a brave and glorious thing to set the world at defiance; to despise its laws; to beard its tyrants; to win power and wealth with your own strong hand; to be no slave of a social system that bows your neck with a yoke of restraint, that tames your hot passions, destroys your natural instincts, but to be a free and independent rover as I am? What matters, if the serfs of society brand you as a thief, a pirate, a murderer, when the fools quake at your very name, and surrender up their riches to your superior bravery?"

"If all men were of that mind, senor, there would be nothing in the world but plundering, bloodshed, and strife."

"You are a provoking fool!" cried the pirate. "What is there in life worth striving for, worth possessing, but the wealth and pleasures that gratify desire?"

"There is honour, conscience, love, friendship, senor," suggested Jack, boldly.

"Que bocado! What a mouthful!" leered the pirate. "Then I take it, although I am captain of a free ship, the monarch of a devoted band, who live or die upon my smiles and frowns; though I have a treasure cave crammed with the spoils of all nations; though I have been victor in a hundred fights, you do not consider me a hero?"

"A hero!" cried Jack, with a burst of irrepressible scorn.

"And yet, in your novels and poems, such men as I are represented as all that is dashing and romantic," laughed the pirate.

"I, for one, was never deceived by such books," returned Jack, fearlessly. "And yet I have delighted to read stirring tales of fights with robbers and pirates."

"And why, pray?"

"I suppose from the same reason that I like to read of daring encounters with tigers, wolves, and other pests and vermin," cried Jack, who again thought of his murdered shipmates, and felt half ashamed of himself for living at the tyrant's sufferance.

"You whelp, it is despair that makes you so audacious," growled the pirate, with a bitter sneer; "but enough, I make you a fair offer; you must lay aside these foolish notions; must enrol your name on my books, and become my follower and a pirate! Or, by San Felipe, my patron saint, you shall die in torments. Your answer?"

"Become an accursed pirate! Never!" shouted our true hero. "I would be burned alive first!"

"Malrya," thundered the pirate, leaping up, his face blazing with fury, and his sword flashing from its sheath. "Out of my sight! or I shall hack you to pieces. Away! And repeat that answer at your peril."

Jack gave a lofty, heroic glance at the villain, and calmly walked away.

CHAPTER IX.

AMBROSE WARNS JACK RUSHTON.

ALONG the silver sands that bordered the golden main, beneath the fragrant groves of palms, mangroves, and breadfruit trees, our hero strode pensively.

He had not proceeded far before his steps were arrested by his beholding a picturesque group of pirates seated upon a coral reef that jutted out into the rippling sea.

He turned aside with loathing and disgust, and plunged into the dense, luxuriant forest, where he might be alone.

He came to a beautiful glade—a spot as lovely as the bowers of paradise—an elysium of bloom and brightness; here he paused, and threw himself under the shade of a gigantic tree.

A foamy waterfall sparkled down from a hollow rock, that might have served as a grotto for the wood-nymphs or fairies, and filled the air with its gushing melody.

Birds, like winged gems, twittered past, and the branches over head rang with the various joyous cries of their multiform colonists.

Soothed by the refreshing sounds, and cooled by the brackish air that wafted from the open, bounding main, poor Jack leaned his head against the gnarled trunk of the vast tree, and suffered the tears to course each other down his brave, though boy-like face, relieving the anguish that filled his heart to overflowing.

His thoughts flew homewards.

Closing his eyes, he gave himself up to the sway of fancy.

So vividly did the dear images present themselves to his imagination that, for awhile, he forgot all his perils and sufferings in the pirates' lair, and he drank in the sweet music of the loved, familiar voices.

Once more he was sporting with his young companions beneath the rook-haunted elms, near the old homestead; the calm and glorious sun of his own dear land—so different from the flaming despot of the tropic skies—was placidly sinking to rest behind the dusky wood-crowned hills, his parting beams barring the dewy sward with the lengthening shadows of the triple wickets, while the young moon floated up through the purpling ether, and the fleecy clouds streaked the heavens, as motionless as if painted on their blue field. Then he saw the face of his mother, and heard her mild voice speaking gentle words.

His own quiet room—the shelf that held his scanty, but well selected library—his little white bed, the white curtains waving in the cool evening air—the little vase of flowers—his linnet at roost in the cage he had made with his own hands—the bible that lay upon the stand of the swing glass.

A cloud blotted out the peaceful dream—a cloud of fire and smoke; dark, evil eyes, glared on him; he started, and stared about him half bewildered.

The blaze of the tropic sun; the dazzling splendour of tropic vegetation; the burning passions of the fiery zone!

Alone in the Pirates' Lair.

He started to his feet and pressed his hand to his throbbing brow.

Then he sank upon his knees, and clasping his hands fervently, breathed a supplication for heavenly help and guidance through the dreadful ordeal to which he was exposed.

As those holy and touching words of the divinest of prayers flowed from his heart—"Lead us not into temptation, but deliver us from evil," he raised his tear-streaming eyes, and a radiant smile, like the sunlight bursting through April clouds, lit up his honest face with all the pure and saintly courage of a martyr; his breast swelled, his boyish form dilated, and his brave eyes shone with a calm, clear light.

He was startled by a deep sigh.

Turning sharply round, he saw the sombre face of Ambrose looking upon him with mingled respect and pity.

The sailor laid his broad, hard hand on the boy's shoulder.

" You are in evil case, my lad," said the pirate in a grave voice. " The senor has sent me to fetch you; are you ready with an answer ?"

" Yes," returned Jack, drawing a deep breath, " I am ready; I am prepared to die."

" Avast ! you must not be rash. You must temporise with the senor. What can you do ? You are in the tiger's den, and at the mercy of a man compared with whom wild beasts are mild and gentle. Do not throw away your life ; think of your mother. Say and do whatever he wishes, and I will take care that you shall not be put upon any service that will go against your conscience."

" Why should I live when all my brave messmates are lying at the bottom of the sea, murdered by this ruthless villain ? No, Ambrose, I cannot perjure my soul by swearing a false oath to serve such a monster ; I would rather perish."

" Then I cannot save you," returned the pirate, gloomily.

" No; but you may do what I asked you at first," said the boy with eagerness. " You do not quail at shedding blood ; do not let those wretches torture me. I am but a weak boy, and my resolution may fail me under the agonies they inflict upon their victims. Kill me, Ambrose ; put a shot through my heart rather than let me die in torment."

"Are you firm in your resolve?"

"Yes, firm!" said the boy. "I have prayed to Heaven for strength to support me through this trial, and I feel that I am equal to it."

Ambrose pondered for a moment.

He suddenly looked up with a bright gleam in his black eyes.

"Give me your hand, lad. I will try to save you; but you must swear one thing."

"What is that?"

"If you escape to one of the other islands, a ship may pick you up; you may get to England, lad. I feel a confidence that one so brave and honest will receive special protection from above. When you reach England ——"

Then he paused and gulped down the qualm in his throat.

"When you reach England," he continued, in a hoarse voice, "it may chance that you will meet *him*—I mean Captain Varney, and her—my Marion; they must never know that Mark Ambrose turned pirate; do ye heed me, lad?"

"Yes; and faithfully give you the promise you require," replied Jack.

"That's well; I know I can trust you. Never mention my name to any one; unless, indeed, to your mother alone. A mother's heart will find excuses for the man who saved her son. But now I must begone."

"Shall I stay here?"

"No; come with me to the top of the rock—crouch low beneath these rushes. Now—you see yon bluff, that stands out to nor'ard?"

"Yes."

"Beneath it you will find a canoe hid in the cave—that dim speck on the sky-line is another island. The canoe is light, you can easily launch her. Steer for the island, and await me there. God speed!"

"But you? Do not you run much risk in thus befriending me?"

"Avast! I will tell the senor that I could not find you—that you were gone when I reached this spot."

"But there will be a pursuit?"

"Trust me to mislead the pursuers; but make all sail, and reach the island before the tide turns. Here, take this pistol with you, and this cartouche; it contains a dozen rounds. Use them sparingly, and do not fire, for your life, till you reach the other islands. Good-bye, lad."

The pirate turned, and, waving his cap, rushed from the spot.

For a few moments Jack lingered, and glanced after him, then he sped away through the rustling forest, crushing the flowers beneath his flying feet.

CHAPTER X.

MORE CASTAWAYS.

OUR scene changes to another of the group of palmy islands that gem the fair Pacific.

Under the brow of a precipitous cliff, a little girl is sitting upon a bank of sand, while at the water's edge, a little distance from her, a tall and well-made negro is busily employed in lashing together a number of spars and timbers, evidently the debris of some wrecked ship, in order to form a raft.

The girl, a lovely little creature, might have been taken for one of the sea-nymphs of the enchanted isle, as she sat, her mild, thoughtful blue eyes gazing afar over the sparkling expanse, her long tresses of glittering gold floating idly in the breeze. Her hands were meekly folded on her lap, which was filled with pearly shells and delicate scarlet sea fern.

The negro was humming to himself in a light-hearted way, as if he were quite forgetful of past horrors and present perils. He worked manfully, hauling along a cask of water which he had drawn from a crystal spring that glittered down the side of the peak.

He placed the cask on the raft, and lashed it firmly.

Another barrel he filled with yams, bananas, limes, and other tropical fruit, and then, having completed his arrangements, he came grinning to the side of the child.

" Come, lilly missee," he said, placing his strong ebon arm round her waist, " dat ole catamaran he carry um to t'other island; de cuss pirate nebber catch um dar, missee, yo make sure ob dat, and by-'m by, come big Englis ship, take um home to de old country. Why fo' you cry, missee? Pa, he gone up yon', he look down on you, he know dat ole Pomp nebba leave yo, dat yo spared fo' purpose go England and see friends, and be good little girl, so ebbery body lub yo like pa and mama. Dey're gone to de bright skies befo' yo, but dey can see yo' and watch ober yo', and will keep near yo' till reach home; and get home berry soon Missie Nell; trust ole Pomp for dat, yah! dat troof !"

"Oh ! why did papa leave me?" sobbed the child. " I did not want to leave him. The bad men threw him down into the deep sea. I wish I had been in his arms. Oh ! let me go to him."

" No, no; missee must go home wid ole Pomp."

" I would rather stay here near papa," sighed the little girl. " I shall not like home, it will be so sad and so cold. There are many pretty shells here, many beautiful flowers, let us wait here; perhaps papa will come again.

The tears sprang to the negro's eyes.

Still the poor faithful fellow laughed with forced gaiety.

"Oh! let us stay!" murmured the little one, imploringly.

"Hi! look dar, missee, dat purty; by gum! dat *are* purty."

And with this emphatic explanation, he pointed at a glittering bevy of flying fish darting like silver arrows from wave to wave.

The girl smiled through her tears, and gave a faint cry of delight.

"An' most curis ting, missee, dis shell. Yo see dem booful colours jes' like de rainbow? Now dis here shell, missee, make such funny moosic—yah! yah!—jes' like de noise ob de sea. Berry curis dat. Yo listen to 'um; dat de reg'lar sea-roar. Hark!"

He pressed the shell to the child's ear.

She smiled witchingly, and her pretty eyes dilated with child-like wonder.

Pompey then began to hum a plaintive negro melody.

Nellie prattled and plied him with many eager questions.

He answered very curtly and inattentively, but with much pleasant humour, keeping on chanting his monotonous lay all the time.

At length the little one talked herself to sleep, and sunk on his breast.

A broad smile passed over the negro's face, and he lifted the slumbering child tenderly in his arms, and carried her to the raft.

Laying her down upon his jacket, and some folded sail-cloth, he pushed off the catamaran.

Running knee deep into the water, he sprang upon the raft, and seized the timber which was to serve as an oar.

He skilfully steered his frail raft over the placid sea.

He had already rounded a rocky promontory of the island, when he suddenly uttered a loud, wild yell.

Startled from her slumber, little Nellie rose, and clung to his knees in an agony of fright.

The negro swayed the oar round his head.

With a fierce, derisive shout, a row-boat manned by Don Pablo, and a dozen of his associate villains, shot out from a little shady cove, and bounding through the water, crashed against the raft.

Don Pablo aimed a pistol at the negro's head, and placed his foot upon the raft.

Nellie shrieked.

Pompey struck madly at the pirate with the oar, through a cloud of fountain spray, which swamped the catamaran.

The bullet from the pirate's pistol would, undoubtedly, have passed through the negro's brain, but for the sudden swamping of the catamaran.

Stumbling along the half-submerged raft, Don Pablo made a clutch at the child.

Still piteously screaming, the poor little girl clove to the negro.

The pirate chief staggered, and tried to balance himself on the swaying raft.

Pompey whirled the oar round his head, and brought it down with a crash upon the pirate's brow.

Don Pablo tossed up his arms, and, reeling backwards, fell plash into the seething waves.

His men immediately fired a volley at the negro.

But the rocking of the boat prevented them from taking steady aim.

The negro ducked his woolly head. Snatching up the child he made a bold spring into the surf.

The next instant he was struggling wildly to reach the shore, which was not far distant, as a headland spurred out from the rocks far into the sea, and the collision had taken place right abreast of this reef.

In their consternation at the sudden disappearance of their leader, who had sunk beneath the waves, the pirates glanced around them with straining eyes.

They uttered a shout at perceiving him floating, apparently senseless, about half a cable's length from the stern of the boat.

They put about, and pulling might and main, reached him and hauled him over the gunwale.

They laid him down in the boat.

His eyes were closed and his features rigid.

His cheeks were pale, their death-like whiteness just tinged by an olive hue.

His long black tresses—for so indeed they might be called, for they were long and soft as a woman's—strewed his shoulders in wet masses; the wound in his forehead had opened, and was clotted with a crimson patch.

His black, fine moustache quivered, and his white teeth were clenched hard.

" Ave Maria purissima !" cried one of the Spaniards, crossing himself. " El capitan is dead !"

" Yha-a !" growled Mutanza the Co-rimante, " den why yo not kill dat black niggar ?   See, him run 'long rocks, him reach de shore !   He make fo' wood, yar nebba catchee him den.   Top him—fiar !   Buccra lubber ! why yo not fiar ?"

One of the pirates, a slim, dark-skinned Spaniard, deliberately rose and picked up a musket that lay across the thwart.

Pomp, with the child in his arms, was now discerned flying like the wind along the shore, and madly bounding from rock to rock.

The Spaniard poised the gun, and kept his keen black eyes upon the negro, awaiting his chance for a shot.

" Maldito ! (Curses !) Fire at him !" shouted the pirates.

The Spaniard raised the gun to his shoulder.

He took steady aim.   He fired.

The white cloud of smoke soared upwards.

The negro was seen stooping on his hands and knees.

The pirates uttered a yell of vindictive triumph.

The next instant Pompey was seen rising to his feet.   He darted behind the rocks, still clasping the little girl in his arms.

An exclamation of rage and disappointment burst from the pirates.

" He has escaped !"

" Es verdad," returned the marksman, revealing himself, " it is true ; but we shall catch him to-night ; he cannot get away from the island.   But let us look to the senor."

Bending over their leader, with anxious and excited features, the swarthy ruffians loosened his shirt collar, and scooping up water in their palms, dashed it on his face.

For some time Don Pablo gave no signs of returning consciousness.

At length he opened his quivering lids, and his bloodshot eyeballs glared around with a vacant look, and a hiss, expressive of acute pain, passed through his gnashing teeth.

"Ay Dios!" he groaned, "it is my wound. But have you killed the black dog?"

"No, senor," returned the pirates, respectfully, "he has escaped to the island."

"Put in shore. I will send a party to take him at once." Then he fell backwards. "Ay de mi! the black villain has killed me."

He fainted. The boat was rowed to shore. The chief was lifted out and carefully borne to the cave.

CHAPTER XI.

INEZ.

A LARGE group of the pirate's followers gathered round the couch on which their chief was laid. Fra Valdez, the priest and physician of the gang, was sent for. He bled the patient, and applied the needful restoratives.

Don Pablo recovered his consciousness, and in an hour, though still faint and pale as death, reclined gracefully upon the divan.

He called for a cup of wine.

He drank eagerly, for his lips were parched with thirst.

"Has Ambrose returned?" he asked.

"Not yet, senor."

"Ha!"

Then he pointed to a gilded table that stood in a corner of the cave.

"Bring me that mirror."

One of the pirates fetched a small looking-glass beautifully mounted in ivory.

He gazed at the reflection of his haggard features for some moments with a grim smile.

Then he handed back the mirror, and with a sigh of exhaustion stretched himself on the couch.

"Padre," he said, with a ghastly leer, "this accident has made a woful change in my appearance. I look like some poor wretch smitten with the vomito—the yellow fever. But come, I must change my clothes. Sancho, bring me my dressing gown."

His orders were obsequiously obeyed.

In a few moments he was wearily reclining upon the couch, wrapped in a costly robe of Indian silk interwoven with gold thread-work.

He lighted a cigarette, and waving his hand, desired all but Fra Valdez to depart.

The pirates vanished, except Sancho, who lingered in hesitation.

"What now?" asked the chief, sharply.

"Senor, a stranger has arrived."

Don Pablo started up with a wild and savage look.

" A stranger ? " he gasped.

Sancho quailed beneath the stern glance, and was too frightened to speak for some time.

" I thought I would tell you at once, senor," he stammered at last, "that a stranger was of the party—but Pedrillo is come."

" But *one* stranger, ha ? " said the pirate, wonderingly ; "and the rest are pirates' comrades ; and in what sort of vessel did they arrive ? "

" In a polacca, senor," returned Sancho. " The stranger desired me to give you this ring, and requests a private audience."

Don Pablo took the ring, which was set with a splendid emerald.

" Muy ben ! " he said, coolly, but with a dark frown of deep vexation ; "admit the stranger. But stay—my pistols ; and keep guard without the entrance of the cave. Send the stranger hither."

Sancho bowed and left the chamber.

" Diablo ! " gasped the pirate, when alone, peevishly flinging away his cigarette. " I always foreboded this ; it will bring no good—if——"

Here his soliloquy was interrupted by the entrance of the stranger, wrapped closely in a large black mantle, who approaching, sank at his feet. The hood fell back, and in all its supreme loveliness the face of a most beautiful woman looked up yearningly at the pirate's piercing eyes.

" Donna Inez de Manilla ! " cried the pirate, in half surprise and complete chagrin.

The lady wove her finely moulded arms about his neck and pillowed her massy raven tresses on his shoulder.

" Si, si, Pablo," she murmured, fondly. " Yes, yes, Pablo ; your own Inez, your wife ! "

The pirate clasped her to his breast, but at the same time bit his lip, and his brow wrinkled with regret and annoyance.

" Que dice ? What say you ? " she asked in endearing accents. " Is not your poor little Inez welcome then ? "

" Si, you are welcome, Inez, mi querida—Inez, my dearest," sighed the pirate ; " but yet I could have wished——"

The girl hastily tore herself from his embrace, her soft cheek suffused with rich crimson, her glorious black eyes glowing with passionate fire.

" Pablo, am I not your wife ? " she gasped. " Are you false to me ? "

Then, for the first time, she noticed the gash on his brow, and the pallor and haggard expression of his face.

With a slight shriek she started back, and then, flinging herself upon his breast, clasped him fervently.

" You are ill, you are wounded," she murmured, her voice broken with sobs ; " and I so thoughtless, so unkind. Ah, forgive me ; forgive me ! "

The pirate frowned, drew a deep breath, yet suffered his hand to rest affectionately on her head.

The rattle of muskets was heard without. Don Pablo started up.

" Poco tiempo—a moment, love," he said, with ill-repressed impatience.

Then he shouted.

" Ho ! there. Is that Ambrose returned ? "

" Si, senor," returned Sancho, entering.

AMBROSE GRIPPED HIS PISTOL, AND CAST A WATCHFUL GLANCE AROUND.

"Tell him to come in."

The man bowed and retired.

Ambrose entered the cave.

His sullen face wore a gloomy look, and he stood stolidly gazing upon the pirate.

Don Pablo munched the ends of his long moustache; he was bursting with spleen, and wanted some one on whom to vent his ill humour.

"Well, Ambrose," he asked, sternly, "where is your prisoner?"

"We have failed in our attempts to find him, senor," said the Englishman, calmly. "Better luck to-morrow."

"This has been a fair day's work," sneered the pirate. "First the insolent English whelp escapes; then I am nearly killed by a cursed black fellow, who, with the child, no doubt the daughter of the captain of our last prize, gets off to the woods; and then——"

He turned a gloomy look upon Inez.

But she did not see that black scowl.

Her arm rested trustingly on her husband's shoulder, and she gazed, smiling, at the Englishman.

"Traitor! you have connived at the boy's escape," cried the pirate, fiercely. "It is useless to deny it."

The Englishman smiled faintly and with supreme indifference at this speech, and shrugged his broad shoulders.

"Patience, senor," he said; "I warrant I'll overhaul him to-morrow."

"Mentira! liar!" growled the pirate, and he grasped the butt of his pistol.

Inez laid one hand on the pirate's and gently drew him back; with the other she waved Ambrose off.

"Escape! begone!" she said, with a silvery laugh, and a look sweet enough to have bewitched St. Antony. "We are old friends, Ambrose; I have not forgotten the service you rendered me when you rescued me from the convent at Luzon. I am sure Don Pablo esteems you, cannot doubt of your fidelity. He is out of temper to-night; his wound has made him impatient. Good night."

A subtle leer of malice curled the pirate's thin lip, and his eyes still glared with subdued anger.

Ambrose well knew the import of that fiendish glance.

Sinking on one knee, he kissed the lady's hand.

Then rising and bowing carelessly, and preserving the same impassible, sullen look which always characterized his dark, saturnine face, he walked calmly forth into the dazzling moonlight.

The great phantom moon blazed like a ball of molten silver in the deep azure sky.

The land glared and the sea flashed in her cold, but intensely brilliant beams.

Ambrose stole along the shore till he came to the mouth of a little river which emptied itself into the sea.

More than once he had been stopped by the various sentinels that guarded the coast.

Ambrose mounted to the top of a high rock, from whence he could command a prospect of the greater part of the island.

The landscape outspread beneath him

was intersected by gleaming pools and silvery streams.

Ambrose descended from the height, and made his way to the mouth of the river.

Beneath an overhanging rock lay a canoe, half buried in the sedges. The pirate dragged it to the water's edge and shoved it off.

Springing in, he seized the paddle, and working it as deftly as an Indian boatman, travelled along the glassy stream, pausing from time to time, and gazing watchfully round.

CHAPTER XII.

SNAP.

THROUGH the dense forest our hero journeyed till he reached the coast on the opposite side of the island.

More than once his steps had been arrested by the faint echo of a distant shout, and several times he had been startled by the crack of a gun shot.

Still he hurried on.

The shore was very wild and grand; huge boulders and masses of rock lay scattered broadcast on all sides; the cliffs were covered with feathery palms, and the sea broke against the rifted strand with greater violence than on the less rugged parts of the isle.

Jack, who was weary after his long, rough walk, threw himself down upon the sands for a rest.

The day was well advanced, and the declining sun glowed through a lurid sky.

Jack's gaze wandered across the sea of molten crimson and rested anxiously upon the hazy bluish speck upon the far sky line which was to be his haven of refuge.

For some time he remained so absorbed in his painful meditations, that he appeared to forget the object of his journey; but suddenly a recollection of the pirate's warning flashed across his mind. The tide was already on the turn, and dense masses of cloud were blowing up on all quarters of the horizon. The night would be dark; he had a long distance to row before nightfall, and there was a danger of his losing his reckoning.

Just as he was about to rise, a startling sound fell upon his ear.

It was the loud barking of a dog.

Jack turned in astonishment.

A dog of the retriever kind, gaunt, and apparently half-starved, came bounding towards him.

Jack could not repress a shout of joy at recognising in the animal his old favourite and playmate Snap, a dog which had belonged to poor Captain Transom.

It would be hard to say whether the lonely boy or the poor animal displayed most delight at their unlooked-for rencontre. In the excess of his joy, Jack fairly hugged the faithful creature, who licked his hands and fawned upon him with boundless affection.

"Come, Snap, my dear old fellow," said the mid, as he patted the dog's rough coat; "since we have met so strangely, it shall take much to part us, eh?"

The dog, who no doubt fully understood the purport of this speech, barked and frisked about with much joyousness.

"Down, sir," cried Jack, shaking his fist. "You must think much and say little in this place, you rascal—we are in the Pirates' Lair. But come, Snap, let us get aboard, for we've a long voyage before us; we must reach yon isle before nightfall, Snap, and I trust in Heaven that it may prove the first stepping-stone to Old England."

So saying, Jack rose, and walking along the shore, looked about him in search of the lofty peak which Mark Ambrose had pointed out to him.

He found beneath a vast cavern, such as Ambrose had described, and entering he discovered the canoe moored in a little stream which poured through the cave into the sea.

Jack found that the boat contained a small barrel of gunpowder, a canister of bullets, and a canvas bag packed with some preserved meat.

It was evident that Ambrose had recently visited the place, and that he had for some days formed a project of escaping from the pirates.

With a grateful heart Jack breathed his prayerful thanks for these good means for deliverance, and opening the bag threw some meat to the dog, which poor Snap devoured with ravenous appetite.

Then jumping into the canoe, the dog sprang nimbly after him, and Jack shoved off with the paddle.

The current was strong, and our hero had much to do to keep his frail bark clear from collisions.

However, the light canoe shot down the stream, and in a few moments the little craft was lightly bounding over the breast of the broad Pacific, propelled by the brave boy's strong and sinewy arms.

CHAPTER XIII.

THE ISLE OF REFUGE.

OVER the heaving waves the light canoe danced along, the white foam wreaths curling in her wake.

Snap lay down in the bottom of the boat, and fell asleep.

Jack's heart fluttered with excitement and anxiety.

There was a savage scowl in the clouds to northward, and the sun shone red and fierce.

If a storm should rise would the frail bark live even an instant in the angry seas?

It was more than doubtful.

And then, in these climates, the darkness falls so suddenly.

If night should come on before he could make the island!

Jack cast a glance over his shoulder.

He was nearing the island of refuge, while the Pirates' Lair was in the distance.

Cheered by this survey of his position, Jack worked with a hearty good will.

Though his arms ached, and huge beads of perspiration started from his brow, he paddled away with untiring resolution.

The sun's glowing disc now touched the horizon.

Jack was abreast of the island.

But to land in the dark on such a rocky and precipitous coast!

Nerved to desperation, he strove might and main to reach the shore.

At length, to his great joy, he found himself driven up the beach by the foaming breakers, the harsh shingles grating under his frail canoe.

He sprang out, knee deep in water, and Snap, rousing from his slumbers, gave a short, joyous bark, and bounded after him.

Jack hauled the boat up beyond the water-line, and dragged it under cover of a weedy rock.

The sun had now sunk in the dark bosom of the sea, and the sky flickered with a lurid glare as of the fitful light of an expiring lamp.

Jack took one look over the sea, and then walked inland.

The scenery was wild and rugged; the island appeared to be intersected by a range of rocky hills, clothed almost to their summits with luxuriant tropical vegetation.

But Jack had little time for further observation.

The flickering glare in the sky faded away, and for a while there was deep darkness, but the heavy pile of clouds grandly parted, and the moon glared forth in silvern glory.

Jack, who, during the temporary darkness, had seated himself under the cliffs, now rose and proceeded on his way inland.

He mounted a rocky causeway, which led into a dark ravine, formed by a rift in the cliffs.

Here he found a cave, and, entering it, stretched himself along the ground in hopes of snatching a few hours' sleep, for he scarcely expected that Ambrose would arrive before morning, and was unwilling to leave the promontory of the island in which he had landed lest he should miss him.

Two or three hours lagged heavily by.

Jack courted sleep in vain, and as the moon shone still brightly, he resolved to leave the cave, and venture to the end of the dark valley, behind which rose a high hill from whence he might command an extensive view of the island.

He rose, and, whistling Snap, walked along the dark glen.

The rocks on either hand were high and beetling, and, being crowned by large, umbrageous trees, formed a sort of tunnel, that was very gloomy.

Jack scrambled along over the rocks, making for the hill beyond the ravine.

This mount lay bathed in the bright moonshine, and, seen through the huge arch of the ravine, resembled the bright

MARK AMBROSE.

picturing of a magic lantern upon a darkened screen.

Suddenly Snap, who followed close upon his master's heels, stopped, and gave a low, fierce growl of warning.

A black and shadowy form loomed out through the gloom at a few paces a-head.

"Hold!" cried Jack, his heart jumping with panic fright—for a sudden surprise in the dark will startle the strongest nerves. "Who goes there? Speak quickly, or I'll fire!"

With this threat he took a backward step, and, drawing his pistol, cocked the trigger with a loud click.

"Belay," grumbled a well-known voice. "'Tis I, hearty—Mark Ambrose!"

"Bravo!" cried Jack, heartily; "I did not expect you would come till the morning."

"If I had stayed till then, it is most likely I should never have come at all," returned Ambrose, grimly. "But come, give me your hand; I will lead you through this pass to my fastness in yonder mountain."

Jack readily clasped the pirate's hand.

Snap, however, did not seem to take much liking to his new acquaintance.

He sniffed at his heels, yelping and snarling in a very unfriendly manner.

"What cursed dog is this?" growled the pirate, instinctively feeling for his knife.

"Don't hurt him, Ambrose," murmured Jack, with a shudder; "he is my faithful Snap; I found him on the shore of the Pirates' Island. He be-

longed to poor Captain Transom; he must have escaped from the wreck."

"See how the brute shrinks from me, with every sign of abhorrence," whispered Ambrose, in a hoarse voice. "There is an instinct in these animals that recoils from the taint of blood; he knows it—he knows what I am!"

"Folly and superstition," returned Jack, with a faint smile. "You are a stranger as yet, but he will soon know you. Here, Snap, good dog; here, sir; this is my friend and preserver. Snap, you must not growl at my friends."

But Snap was not to be conciliated.

He gave a short snarl, and bounded off for some distance—then followed sullenly.

"Humph! and it seems you and your dog are not the only pair that reached the island in safety," returned Ambrose.

"What, have any of my messmates escaped?" cried Jack, with eagerness and wonder.

"So I hear; the captain's black servant with a little girl."

"Nellie Transom!" cried Jack, jumping for joy; "but where are they?"

Ambrose gave our hero an account of Don Pablo's attack upon the raft, and Pompey's escape with the child; but added,

"They are sure to be taken; yet there is one chance for the little one."

"I hope so; monster as that Pablo is, he spared me, and will not find the heart to kill such a pretty little darling as Nellie is."

"Would the wild beasts in the forest spare her for her innocence and beauty?"

sneered Ambrose. " Don Pablo has the heart of a tiger."

" And yet you say there is a chance for her."

" A very poor one. Donna Inez may see her and intercede for her."

" Donna Inez ? Who is she ?"

" Don Pablo's wife."

" His wife ! Can such a wretch have a wife ?"

" Aye, lad, and a glorious beauty she is, and loves him with all the fiery passion of her Spanish blood," returned Ambrose.

" His wife ! While telling his hideous adventures he never mentioned her," said Jack.

" He never does," rejoined the other, " and I'll warrant her visit to the island is about as welcome to him as the arrival of a man-of-war with a mission to destroy him."

" But who is she ?"

" The daughter of Don Francisco de Luzon, the governor of Manilla."

" But how did he gain her love ?"

" 'Tis a long story, but it amounts to this—Don Pablo went ashore at Manilla under the disguise of a merchant ; he was presented to the governor, who invited him to his house. There he met Donna Inez, and soon won her heart by his blandishments, as he is a splendid-looking fellow, and has the stamp of high caste imprinted upon his evil, but handsome, countenance, and, moreover, appeared to be immensely rich ; her father raised no objection against the match, and the pair were accordingly married with great ceremony. It was agreed that Donna Inez should go on board her husband's ship, which he said

was bound for Spain, but on the very eve of her departure the real character of the bridegroom was discovered by a rejected suitor of the bride. Don Pablo was immediately arrested and thrown into prison, but by my aid and the band's he was rescued."

" And did the lady still cleave to him ?"

" Aye, and would have fled with him, but was detected and seized as she was leaving her father's house. The old noble was fearfully enraged, and compelled the unfortunate girl to enter a convent, from which we afterwards carried her off ; but again she fell into the hands of her relations. Her father meanwhile had died, and her uncle had been appointed governor in his place ; he was a kind old man, and received his niece to his home on her promise that she would not attempt to escape."

" But she has not kept her promise ?"

" Why, it would seem a party of spies belonging to our gang are always stationed at Manilla ; she persuaded some of these fellows to bring her to the island."

" Do you think the wretch cares for her ?"

" I believe that he loves her as much as is possible to one of his ungovernable, selfish, and false nature : he is growing weary of her, though, I can see that—the result will be some tragedy, for she is as jealous and impetuous as she is fond and devoted ; but let it pass, lad ; I have done with the gang for ever."

" That's well said, my hearty," returned Jack. " Who knows but out of all this evil good may come ?"

"To you, perhaps, but not to me," sighed the pirate. "I am beyond the pale of hope; I desire no more than just to see you embarked in some vessel homeward bound, and then I can die."

"Never say *die!*" laughed Jack. "There are bright days in store for you yet, Ambrose."

"The shadows of the past would darken the brightest future," returned the pirate, moodily, "but bring to—here is our hiding place."

Ambrose led our hero into a cavity in the side of the mountain screened by a large mass of rock.

The pirate bade him lie down and rest himself while he mounted guard.

Jack would have objected to this arrangement, and have insisted upon going on sentry himself, but he was outworn and could scarcely keep his eyes open; so, with a few words of thanks and encouragement to his friend, he threw himself down, and was soon sunk in a profound and dreamless slumber.

CHAPTER XIV.

THE ATTACK.

Jack started from his sleep.

His dog was growling.

Ambrose stood at the entrance of the little cavern, which he had closed by rolling down an immense stone from the hill side.

The pirate held a pistol clutched in his right hand, and listened breathlessly at the crevice between the stone and the rocks, through which the pale golden beams of morning were richly streaming.

"What is it, Ambrose?" whispered our hero. "Are we pursued?"

"Aye; stopper all," grunted the pirate, without taking his ear from the door. "Silence that cursed dog!"

Jack spoke to Snap, who crouched at his feet, and stretched out his head on the ground, and kept his watchful eyes fixed on the entrance.

A shout was heard in the woods below.

Then the clear ringing voice of Don Pablo himself was heard issuing orders in an imperious tone to his men.

"We are lost!" cried Jack.

"But we will sell our lives dearly, eh, lad?"

"Yes; in defence of my life, and in warring with such demons, I shall not be over nice," returned Jack, whose bold spirit rose with the occasion. "Look, Ambrose, there is the villain Pablo himself coming up the hill. Stand clear, I will take aim at him through the crevice."

"Avast, lad; reserve your shot till the last. Follow me."

Ambrose ran to the end of the cavern.

The rocks shelved down to a little opening on another side of the hill.

The pirate crawled on hands and knees through the opening.

They found themselves upon a sort of

ledge, or table land, overlooking the valley.

"Away, lad!" cried Ambrose, pausing to see if they were followed from the cave.

A puff of white smoke now burst from the dense foliage below, followed by a loud crack.

Then a loud, derisive yell rang through the forest.

Ambrose staggered back.

With a cry of sympathy and indignation, Jack sprang to his side.

"'Tis nothing, lad," said the seaman, shaking the blood from his brawny arm. "A mere scratch."

Jack instantly bound up the wound with his neckerchief.

"Off!" said Ambrose. "I will follow you."

Jack bounded away like a chamois.

He had not proceeded far, however, before another shot was fired from the valley.

Jack tossed up his arms, stood for a second motionless, reeled, and fell heavily.

"I am struck, Ambrose!" he groaned. "The villains have killed me; but save yourself. Heed not me. Run, man, run."

Ambrose uttered a savage execration.

He fired both his pistols into the wood.

A piercing yell told that they had reached the mark.

Ambrose dragged the wounded boy under cover of some trees, and then reloaded the pistols.

Poor Jack had fainted.

Ambrose threw him lightly over his shoulder, and dashed across the mountains.

As he ascended higher and higher, he was followed by the shouts of his pursuers scrambling after him through the dense wood.

The ascent grew at each step more rugged and precipitous.

Encumbered by his burden, Ambrose found it almost impossible to escape his pursuers. One advantage, however, he possessed, in his knowledge of the country.

He had spent many days exploring it during the absence of Don Pablo and the greater part of his band at Manilla.

Still the shots rattled through the trees; and had they not been fired at such a long range, must have proved fatal.

From time to time Ambrose caught just a glimpse of the pirates; but for the most part they fired from the bush.

Herds of light-footed antelopes bounded before the fugitive, and the macaws and paroquets in the woods screamed their terror.

Ambrose reached a long stony valley, through which ran a clear and silvery stream.

He scrambled to the top of a rock.

Here one of the pirates who had been placed there as sentinel attacked him; but the combat was soon decided in the favour of Ambrose, who shot his assailant through the heart.

Then, grimly seating himself upon the rock, with the fainted boy's head resting on his knee, Ambrose gripped his pistol, and glared down upon the valley with a look that betokened the dogged courage and fortitude of his British nature.

For some time the silence was unbroken. A pair of vultures had perched themselves on the top of a precipice, and stretched out their livid necks, and pierced with their red eyes a ravenous, gloating look upon the dead body of the pirate, and the insensible form of our hero.

Suddenly Ambrose heard a growl and a loud cry. He turned his head.

Knife in hand, the negro Malanza was crouching behind him; but the brave Snap had sprung at his throat and dragged him down.

CHAPTER XV.

THE PURSUIT CONTINUED.

AMBROSE rose and seized the savage negro by the throat.

Jack still remained insensible, and sank upon the earth.

The sturdy Englishman and the tall, wiry black fellow were well matched in strength and endurance.

The struggle between them was fierce, and continued for some moments.

The dog took his share in the conflict.

He fixed his fangs in the calf of the negro's leg, causing him to yell with pain.

At length, Ambrose, twining his arms round the negro's body, lifted him by main force from off the ground, and hurled him down the side of the rock.

He stood for an instant, his eyes glaring, his teeth clenched, gasping for breath, and gazing, with eager scrutiny, along the valley and the tops of the surrounding hills.

He once more lifted the insensible boy in his arms.

He cautiously scrambled down the rock, keeping carefully concealed by the thick vegetation which clothed its sides.

Upon reaching the level of the vale he looked round for the negro.

The body of the Corimante, who was stunned and fearfully wounded from his fall, was just discerned through the leaves of some strange tropic plant of the cactus kind.

Ambrose laid Jack down upon the ground.

He then dragged the negro from out the cover.

The pirate black, who was half naked, had a rich red shawl swathed round his breast, which bristled with quite an armoury of daggers and fire-arms.

Ambrose made free with these, and having already secured the weapons of the other pirate whom he killed, was now formidably armed.

He also cut away a calabash full of brandy from the negro's side, and then once more took Jack up in his arms, and rushed on through the valley.

He reached the hill at the end of the

vale, and toilfully clambering its side, rested at a spot where a pile of massy stones lay heaped as if by the hand of man.

Gently placing the boy upon a bank, he stooped over him, and proceeded to examine the extent of his wounds, and to use what means he had to restore animation.

He found that the shot had passed under Jack's arm, grazing the flesh, but, fortunately, not entering between the ribs, nor even lodging in his side.

But the poor boy had, nevertheless, lost a great quantity of blood, and lay as pale, motionless and ghastly, as if life had departed.

Ambrose tore away the boy's blue shirt, and, twisting a scarf tightly round his body, managed to staunch the wound.

He then brought some water in a dry gourd from a little spring that bubbled up among the rocks hard by, and poured it upon the lad's pale, cold brow.

Forcing open the clenched teeth of his patient, Ambrose poured some drops of the ardent spirits from the calabash into his parched lips.

After a time he was rewarded by seeing the boy's slender frame quiver with a visible tremor, the flush returned to his pale cheeks and brows, and at lenth his eyelids slowly and painfully unclosed, and he glared around with blood-shot eyes.

Jack gave a deep gasp.

He tried to speak, but could not; however, he faintly smiled, and, drooping his head backwards, reclosed his eyes.

Snap, meantime, had shown every mark of distress at his master's case, and had watched his recovery with great anxiety.

Seeing the good results of the treatment Jack received at the hands of his skilful nurse, the dog began to jump, and gambol about in great delight.

" What cheer, lad ?" asked Ambrose, in gruff but kindly tones, while his dark, melancholy countenance softened as he gazed upon the boy. " Don't alarm yourself; your wound is not dangerous. I have had some experience in these matters, and can promise you that you will soon be all right, my hearty. What you want now is a day's rest."

" Thank you, Ambrose," returned Jack, feebly clasping his hand. " Your kindness to a poor, lone castaway will not lose its reward."

" I am rewarded by hearing you speak once more, little cheery," returned the seaman, smiling. " But we are not out of danger yet; one good thing has resulted from that rascally black's attack——"

" The bloodhounds are once more on our track," growled the pirate. " Do you think, Jack, that you can bear removal ?"

" Yes—yes, Ambrose," groaned our hero. " But do not care too much for me; hide me somewhere, and look out for yourself, hearty."

" For myself?" returned the pirate, with a scowl. " But for your sake I would not stir a pace, but would turn at bay upon the hounds, and perish in defending myself. But, come, the shouts grow louder, and the wolfish pack will be in sight directly. We must be gone !"

PERILOUS POSITION OF AMBROSE AND JACK.

With this, he lifted the boy on to his broad shoulder.

Although he was suffering the most acute pain, our brave young hero uttered no cry of complaint, but subdued his anguish with Spartan fortitude.

Once more Ambrose was racing for life or death along the rugged hill-side.

The shouts were heard continuously, growing fiercer and louder, as the pursuers gained upon the fugitives.

"Keep a good look out, my hearty," said Ambrose, as he toiled up the hill.

But Jack returned no answer.

The seaman looked up into his face.

His bodily resources, unable to hold out against the intensity of his sufferings, the poor boy had fainted.

Ambrose paused.

He gnashed his teeth with rage.

There was one thing in his favour—the pursuers, although on the right track, had not yet sighted their chase.

Ambrose looked about him half despairingly.

Just beneath him lay a deep, dark ravine, completely covered in by the dense foliage of the thickset trees and bushes.

Ambrose plunged down into this dingle.

Whistling the dog to his side, he struggled through the prickly shrubs, tearing his clothes and scratching his flesh by contact with a myriad thorny points, and, crouching low down in the sere giant grass, with Jack's head resting upon his knee, and the dog lying stretched by his side, listened intently to every little sound.

The shouts died away.

Nothing was heard but the eternal buzz of insects, the chattering of monkeys, and the shrieks of the macaws and paroquets. Suddenly there was a loud rustle among the leaves, as the foliage rolled like a green and amber sea beneath the wing of a strong, fitful gale.

At that moment Ambrose little thought that there was aught of import to him or to the brave, hapless boy whom he had defended so gallantly in that passing blast; but as the sequel will show, it was destined to save their lives, and, at least for a time, to deliver them out of the hands of their cruel and ruthless enemies.

CHAPTER XVI.

THE BURNING FOREST.

AMBROSE, Jack, and Snap had not lain long concealed before the crackling of boughs and the crush of footsteps betokened the approach of their savage foes.

"I am persuaded, senor," said a voice in Spanish, "that they are hiding in the bush."

Ambrose looked uneasily at the dog. But the sagacious animal lay quite quiet, his head stretched out, and his ears pricked up, his black muzzle resting on his fore paws, watchful, but perfectly still.

"It may be so," returned Pablo, himself; "scour the wood; I will give a hundred piastres to the man that finds them—upon their death or capture, that is—but beware how you let them escape."

"Viva el capitan!" shouted the pirates.

"Jose!"

"Here, senor."

"Clamber to the top of that palmetto, and keep a bright look out."

"Si, senor," returned the man, touching his forelock.

"Take that long carbine from Sancho. If you see the Yenglese dogs, fire at them; your shot will direct the next in their search. Is any one stationed on the brow of the hill?"

"Tomaso, senor, Yangho — the Chinese and the negro Maroquin."

"That will do. Sancho, remain with me; and now away, and return without the prisoners at your peril."

The men dispersed.

Don Pablo reclined beneath a tree, and lighted his cigarette.

"There is one thing I have forgotten, Sancho," said the pirate, addressing his fellow countryman and confederate in villany, who had stationed himself at a little distance, and stood leaning upon his sword.

"What is that, senor?"

"When I offered the hundred piastres for the cursed traitor, Ambrose, and the young British bull-dog whelp, I ought to have attached the condition that they should be taken alive. A pretty trick they have played me; I don't like the idea of giving them easy quittance by a shot or a stab. Ambrose is a fitting subject to be made a terrible example of."

"No doubt they will be taken, senor."

"That is only a matter of time," returned Pablo, coolly, whiffing at his cigarette; "but it would give pleasure to put them to some torment; those meddling, blustering, dogmatic English; how I abhor the whole race!"

"They are a race of heretics, senor."

"Ave Maria!" returned the pirate chief, crossing himself. "You say right; they ought to be exterminated."

There was a pause.

"Que demonio! what is that moving in the bush?" cried the pirate chief, suddenly, pointing towards the ambush of the fugitives.

Ambrose was stealthily crawling away from the spot, dragging Jack along as quietly as he could.

Sancho rushed to the bush, holding a pistol in each hand.

He just caught a glimpse of the dog, who was crouching along in the wake of Ambrose.

"'Tis some wild animal, senor," he said; "an ounce or a wild cat."

"Fire at it," said the pirate chief.

Sancho took steady aim through the dense foliage at the spot where he imagined the creature must be lurking.

He pulled the trigger.

The report of the pistol rung in loud echoes among the rocks.

With a fierce "whit!" the slugs swept over poor Snap's head, and clipped a piece out of his ear.

The poor dog gave a terrific growl, ending in a sharp whine of pain.

But when Ambrose, turning on his hands and knees, shook his fist, the sagacious animal ceased from howling, and cowering down at his side, lay perfectly quiet, though convulsed with pain.

Sancho entered the bush.

But soon he recoiled, driven back by the sharp thorns of the prickly thickets.

"Have you killed the brute?" asked Don Pablo.

"I think not, senor; I saw it crawl away."

"You are a fool," was the polite rejoinder.

Sancho made no reply to this, but submissively returned to his post, and busied himself in reloading his pistols.

At length the pirate chief started up, and stamped his foot with impatience.

"Estrano!—strange," he muttered; "this delay is provoking. Run and hail Jose, and ask him if he has yet sighted the spies."

Sancho retired.

He returned with a long face.

Don Pablo frowned, gnawed his lips, and beat the ground peevishly with his foot.

"He has seen nothing of them?"

"No, senor."

"Muy, estrano—very strange," returned the pirate chief, as he once more seated himself, and stroked his black moustache with an air of intense vexation.

Ambrose was watching him through the leaves, with the glare of a crouching tiger.

"They are but two," he thought, as his fingers curled round the trigger of his pistol. "I might kill them both—but, then, the boy! I should be seen from the tree, from the hills above. No, I will save the boy."

And he thrust his pistols quickly into his belt, as if afraid of keeping them in his grasp, lest his impulse to fire on the miscreants should prevail over his caution.

Again Don Pablo rose, and restlessly paced about.

"Do you think they are in the wood?" said he.

"I feel convinced of that, senor," returned the other.

"Ha, ha! A brave thought, Sancho," laughed Don Pablo, fiendishly. "We will burn them out; the long drought has dried up the foliage, and the forest will burn like tinder. Which way is the wind?"

"The wind has fallen."

"It blew half a gale but now," replied the chief.

"Aye, senor, but veeringly; it seemed to come from all quarters at once," returned the other.

"Enough. Men can be stationed on either side the valley. We will try it, Sancho. Si, si! I am resolved it shall be tried."

So saying, the arch-scoundrel took a silver bugle from his side and blew a long, ringing blast, which, in a short time, brought his followers to his side.

They came straggling in, singly, in pairs, and in groups of four or five.

Ambrose saw that there was not an instant to be lost.

Of course it must be understood that the long chase had occupied a greater part of the day.

The sun had disappeared behind the hills, and the sky at the zenith was darkening fast.

Ambrose glanced upwards.

A little fleecy cloud hung overhead.

At first it seemed motionless.

But, watching it narrowly, the seaman perceived that it was moving.

His experienced eye, judging by the direction in which it moved, guessed from what quarter the coming gale would rise.

With Jack in his arms, and Snap following close upon his heels, he forced his way through the tangled underwood.

Fortunately, as it happened, the return of the pirates, who occasioned a great deal of noise by the clanking of their weapons and their loud execrations at having been foiled in their efforts of capturing their prey, drowned the sound of his retreating footsteps.

He heard the shouts and laughter of the scoundrels as, in obedience to their chief's order, they ran along the skirts of the wood, gathering faggots and bundles of dry grass, and scattering broad-cast the gunpowder from their cartouches.

At length he reached the end of the wood, and stopped to regain breath at the foot of the precipitous rocks.

Looking up, he beheld a number of the lawless miscreants rushing along, yelling like demons, and waving flaming branches about their heads.

He tried to pierce the deep gloom of the forest with his strained eyes, but of course the leafy screen was impenetrable to his glance.

At last he heard the loud, ringing voice of Don Pablo giving orders to his men to set the forest in a blaze.

Then through the dark interstices of the trees bright yellow flashes were seen; a hissing noise, swelling to a loud, fierce crackle, ensued; dense volumes of smoke rolled heavily upwards; the forest was in a blaze.

Then came a long, soughing noise of the rising wind, as if rushing to the scene of mischief, and in less time than it takes to record the fact, the greater part of the dense jungle was in flames!

Then arose a deafening clamour.

Fearful howls of the wild animals frightened from their lairs.

The hiss of serpents, the stunning buzz of myriads of insects which filled the air.

The shrill twitterings, the quailing, the shrieking of numberless birds startled from their roosting places.

The pirates had not taken the precaution of first stationing themselves at their posts of vantage along the rocks, and even if they had done so, the wind blew so fiercely from that side of the jungle where Ambrose was, that his enemies on the other side must have been driven off by the burning torrent of roaring fire that swept towards them.

Even those stationed on the lee side of the jungle, finding themselves among trees—for, though less densely than in the heart of the valley, the vegetation continued almost to the top of the hill —were struck with a sudden panic, and fled towards their companions who were scrambling up the opposite precipice.

Ambrose climbed up the steep rocks till he reached a ridge in the dry bed of a mountain torrent. Here he perched himself, and, holding on by the branch of a tree, gazed over the grand but awful scene.

Below him surged along the yellow-blazing, red-glaring, cloud-vomiting river of roaring flames.

Every branch, every leaf, stood out in intense black relief, or glared with living brightness. Light flakes of fire flew from branch to branch; huge arms of timber smoulder, lurid red, or bent and broken, floated down in charred white ashes into the sevenfold-heated furnace beneath.

Above rolled the black smoke clouds, reflecting on their billowing bases the red glare of the raging flames; here showers of glittering sparks, and pieces of flaming wood, or sprays of foliage shot up or dropped and rattled down; ever and anon the charred trunk of some towering palm, with its crown of flame, tottered, and fell with the crash of a falling column.

Every cranny, and ledge, and corner of the surrounding rocks glared forth with wondrous distinctness in the intense crimson glow.

Added to the sublime terrors that appal the sight, the horrid sounds that distracted the ear were equally awe-inspiring.

Added to the thousand cries of the terrified birds and animals escaping from, or perishing in, the dismal conflagration of their general home, came from time to time the thundrous roar of falling timber; the hissing, seething, and crackling of the burning boughs; the spluttering and spurting of the boiling sap and resin, and the rattle of loosened stones clattering down from the hill-sides.

The very earth seemed to rumble as if shaken by an earthquake.

The heat was stifling. Ambrose's eyes started, and felt as if they had been filled with some heated films; he drew in draughts of heated air that parched his mouth, and sickened him; his clothes became so hot that they seemed instantly on the verge of catching fire.

But still the strong, fierce, but friendly gale drove the flames away from him.

He looked across the fiery torrent, pouring through the beautiful vale.

Afar off, clustered on the side of the hill, the pirates were gathered together.

Their faces flushed bright vermilion, all the varied colours of their garments were blent into one fierce red; their weapons glistened bright as lightning streaks; and there the sea-fiends stood, exulting over their hellish work.

All at once they caught sight of Ambrose, clinging to that lone crag, the boy in his arms, and the dog crouched at his feet.

They uttered their vengeful malice in one deep yell of fury.

Ambrose, excited to a pitch of madness by the dreadful scene, shook his fists at them, and raved his hate and defiance. And then, yielding to a wild impulse, he discharged his pistols at them, of course without effect, as they were far out of range.

Even in that appalling moment, Ambrose could not help noticing how the report of his fire-arms sounded no louder than the snapping of an unprimed fire-lock amid the deafening din.

Suddenly the wind dropped, and the flames, collecting in one glaring mass, soared steadily upwards, and that which before had been a rolling stream of flame, now stood like a high wall of fire, completely hiding the pirates from his view.

Then the wind turned treacherous, and, veering to the opposite quarter, drove the flames towards him. In an instant he seemed struggling in a sea of fire. His limbs faltered, and his skin scorched and blistered. He desperately bounded up the rock.

The long, snake-like flames hissed after him, seizing root and branch in their progress, and seeming to chase him with cruel purpose.

Upwards and upwards he scrambled. From time to time he was forced to rest from exhaustion.

It was not till goaded by the very flame-lances that he could pluck up sufficient energy to push on.

But never, in the most perilous moments, did it enter the mind of the strange, misguided, but not ignoble, mind of the pirate, to abandon the poor boy he had sworn to protect.

At last he reaches the top of the mountain.

On one hand, but far below, roars the gulf of fire.

On the other, stretches out the calm blue deep, tinged with a faint crimson glow, and over it spangle the myriad stars over one half of the calm sky, while the other seems veiled by a murky curtain of smoke and cloud.

CHAPTER XVII.

FEVER-STRICKEN.

MARK AMBROSE stood for some time gazing around him upon the grand and imposing spectacle.

The fire had spread through a narrow pass, and had been caught by a wood in the next valley; the flames could now be seen soaring up behind the dark, bulging hills.

It seemed as if one half of the island were on fire, and that it was more than probable that if the wind continued in the same quarter, the whole would be in flames, for the isle was in every part densely wooded.

Turning his eyes towards the sea, Ambrose beheld the pirates crowding into a large proa and a couple of row-boats, and soon the former spread out its fan-like sail of cocoa matting, and soared away across the bounding main, the row-boats stoutly pulled by the motley gang following in her wake.

Ambrose anxiously watched the sky to see how the wind lay, and then, with a gloomy look, walked down the hill-side and made his way towards the shore.

On his way he picked up the body of a dead bird, evidently recently killed while attempting to escape from the burning forest.

There were many such, scattered about over the hills, and along the beach.

Ambrose picked it up, and gathering some of the tropical fruits that lay beneath many a curious-looking tree, he looked around him in search of one of the numerous caverns with which the rocks and cliffs were mined.

Finding one which he thought would serve his purpose, he entered it.

It was a huge vault, its high roof lost in the black shadow.

He made a bed of leaves and seaweed, on which he placed poor Jack.

Then, collecting some resinous wood, he lighted a fire near the mouth of the cave, and hung the bird upon two cross sticks to cook.

He took a pull from the calabash, and having thus refreshed himself, carefully tended our hero.

To his surprise, he found that Jack was not insensible, though apparently sunk into a heavy stupor.

His limbs were fevered, his lips parched; his hollow cheeks burned with a hectic flush, and his eyes glowed with a burning brilliance, when he at length unclosed them, and gazed wildly around.

He was evidently delirious.

He muttered incessantly, and with the greatest rapidity.

"It is the fever," whispered the pirate, hoarsely, as, with his hands clenched in grief, he gazed upon the boy's distorted and working features. "The boy will die."

"Is that you, Harry? Bring me a cup of water," hissed the boy. "Ha, ha, land! Do you hear that cry? Land ho! Look, Will, there is the old Lizard; soon we shall be sailing up the rare old Thames, and then, hey for home, my hearties! Six bells; starboard watch, ahoy! Tumble up, lads, ha, ha, ha! Oh, for the love of God, one cup of water!"

And the poor lad sank with his head upon the pirate's breast.

Still he muttered, muttered, muttered, as if his tongue would never tire; still he opened his burning eyes, and gazed insanely round, now bursting into a maniacal, hollow laugh, then maundering tearfully.

Ambrose squeezed the juice of limes upon his lips, and then laying his head upon the pillow he had made with his own jacket, he stole out of the cave, and searching among the verdure that mantled the cliffs selected some leaves of a narcotic plant.

These he macerated between two stones, and mixed them with water in a gourd.

Returning to the side of the sick lad, he forced him to swallow some of this mixture.

Soon the soothing medicine began to show its effects, and the poor boy stretched his limbs along the rude bed, and drooping his head, fell into a deep slumber.

Ambrose watched him for some time, and then he walked to the fire.

The bird was by this time roasted, and, tearing it to pieces, the pirate made a meal of it and some sea biscuits he found in his pockets.

He threw a leg of the fowl to Snap, but the faithful dog had placed his head upon his master's breast, and was whining in a low, piteous tone.

He paid no regard whatever to Ambrose's invitation to share with him in the repast, but remained quite motionless and absorbed in sorrow.

Ambrose sat pondering moodily, his arms crossed upon his knees, his eyes fixed intently upon the fire.

From time to time he would rise and give a glance of sympathy at the sleeping boy, go to his side, bathe his brow, part his fair curls, and smooth his pillow.

Once as he gazed longer and more earnestly than usual, a sudden and bitter curse burst from his quivering lips.

He walked moodily to the fire.

"Aye, let it go!" he wailed. "But, O! what might have been but for her falseness! I might have had a boy like this; I might have been free from guilt; and now I am wifeless, childless—a pirate! a murderer!—blood-stained and lost! Yet why should I blame her? How can I blame myself? I was goaded to madness! Ha! there are cases when a man must die to save himself from what is worse than death. Why did I live?"

Passing his fingers through his dark hair, and clenching his teeth to suppress his qualms of inward shame and agony, the guilty man came once more to the side of the innocent boy.

As he stooped beside him, a sudden growl from the dog and a slight noise caused him to turn with a slant.

A pair of black eyes gleamed in through the smoke of the fire.

He sprang to his feet.

In an instant he had seized his pistol.

"What cheer, hearty," cried a gruff voice; "you look like an Englishman, and surely a man that can show such kindness to a poor, sick lad, can't be a landshark altogether; I've watched ye these two minutes. Who are ye, mate? where do you hail from? Do you belong to the 'farnal pirate crew? 'cos if so, mind your eye, that's all, and stand clear, for I'm not without a brace of popguns."

Ambrose was for some moments before he could recover his surprise.

"Why, who are you?" he asked.

"I'm Thomas Hawser, otherwise Old Tom. At your sarvice; late bo'swain of the barque 'Titania,' the cap'en, mates, and crew of which were all butchered by a cursed crew of pirates."

"It is strange, shipmate, but I think

I have seen you before?" said Ambrose, looking the worthy old tar in the face.

"Aye, like enough," returned Tom Hawser, with a frown; "you were of the cutting-out party, belikes."

"No, not I," stammered Ambrose; "but now you tell me your name, I recollect you as an old messmate ———"

"On board the 'Fearless,' under that old shiver-the-mizen Captain Varney! Why, yes. Tip us your flapper, my cheery; I know you—you are my old chum, Mark Ambrose!"

CHAPTER XVIII.

TOM HAWSER'S NARRATIVE OF HIS ESCAPE.

STEADFASTLY regarding each other, Mark Ambrose and Tom Hawser stood silent for some moments.

The honest face of the boatswain of the unfortunate "Titania" wore an expression of mingled pity and reproach, while the pirate's gloomy countenance darkened with sullen ferocity as he caught the meaning of his old messmate's stern and piercing look.

His head drooped upon his broad breast; his arm fell, and he tried to draw back his hand from the other's grasp.

But Tom gripped it fast.

"Avast, old shipmate," he murmured, gruffly. "We're all on us frail creatures; we launches on the high seas, like any other sort o' craft, to sink or swim. Sometimes we gets buffeted about by contrary winds, sometimes we lies becalmed in uncomfortable latitudes; often we strikes on sunken rocks or runs aground on shoals, and some on us sails gaily afore a fair wind, and anchors in prosperous harbours. It's all accordin' to destiny, ye see. Look at us, for instance; I means, in course, us poor chaps as sailed in the 'Titania.' We weighed anchor on a Friday, and what could ha' been expected to result from such a percedin'? What else, my hearty, but jist what happened. Yet, shiver me, messmate, I'd rather have found ye lying all astrand like a sheer hulk than seen ye sailing in fair weather under such 'farnal black colours."

"I've hauled them down, Tom," returned the other, faintly smiling. "I am no longer a pirate."

"Say ye so, mate? Now, that's hearty like," returned the boatswain, in a jolly tone, as he warmly wrung his old friend's hand. "But, tell me, who or what has brought about this good change?"

"He did," returned Mark, simply, as he pointed to poor Jack, who lay writhing on his bed of anguish.

Tom Hawser bounded across the cave, and threw himself upon his knee beside the sick boy.

"My jib!" he cried, in great astonishment, "Why, 'tis our brave little middy, Jack Rushton!"

The dog, under ordinary circumstances so sharp and watchful, had hitherto remained unconscious of the presence of a stranger; his shaggy head rested on his young master's breast, and he seemed absorbed in grief and sympathy.

Now, however, he raised his dark, earnest, eloquent eyes to the old sailor's face, and recognizing him, fawned upon him and licked his hands, with a low, coaxing whine.

"What, Snap, old boy!" cried Tom, patting him. "What, you here, too? But where's your young mistress, eh, old fellow? Where's the darling of our crew; our pet, Nellie Transom?"

The poor brute seemed perfectly to understand what was said, for, uplifting his head, he uttered a long plaintive howl.

The patient now started and raised himself upon his elbow, glaring wildly around him and recommencing his delirious mutterings.

"And so the gallant little chap is wounded?" said the boatswain, pityingly. "How did this come about, Mark?"

Ambrose gave his friend a brief but succinct account of his own and Jack's adventures in the Pirates' Lair, their escape, the wild pursuit, the burning of the forest, and their arrival at the spot where he, the boatswain, had found them.

Tom listened with breathless interest, and regarded Mark as he proceeded with increasing seriousness.

"And now, messmate," said Tom, "since you have brought your queer yarn end to end, tell me what you mean to do?"

"That is soon told," returned Ambrose. "This island is often visited by the Indians in their proas. I can speak their language a little, and can, by means of a few presents, induce them to convey you over to Guajan, the largest of these Ladrone Islands, where there is a Spanish settlement, called San Ignacio de Aganna, whence you may embark for England; meanwhile some vessel may pass which may recognize your signals."

"But yourself, my hearty; you will go with us?"

"Care not for me, messmate," returned Ambrose, gloomily. "If you can save yourself and this poor lad I shall be content."

Tom Hawser would have uttered some cheering remark, but his companion turned sullenly away and busied himself in tending the patient.

He repeated the operation of pounding some medicinal root between two stones, and then mixing it with spirits and water in a cocoa-nut shell.

Jack, refreshed by the soothing draught that Ambrose forced upon him, soon sank into a deep refreshing slumber.

The two men rose, and strolling forth from the cave ascended a hill whence they could command an extensive view of the beautiful island.

On the north side, and at about a league from shore, towered upwards from the deep blue sea, through the amber sky, the tall, romantic peak of a large reef called Saypan.

To the south was seen the bluish hills of the Pirates' Isle.

The country beneath them was richly diversified; here, chains of lofty moun-

THE PURSUIT OF POMP.

tains, some of them volcanic, their summits riven with yawning craters; there, wide spreading plains, on which vast herds of wild cattle were grazing, or wading through the numerous pools that flashed like mirrors in the sun glow.

The bases of the hills and the beds of the valleys were thickly grown with curious tropical trees and plants—cocoa-palms, guavas, lemons, oranges, and, most remarkable of all, the stately "rhymay," or bread-fruit tree—which somewhat resembles the elm, is about the same height, and presents the same venerable aspect; the leaves of this curious and useful tree are large, glossy, and of a dark green hue, the edges curiously indented. The fruit is heart-shaped, about the size of a child's head, and, when roasted, forms an agreeable and nutritious food. In the distance a thin cloud of blue smoke soared upwards from the still smouldering forest, resting in a long, dark cloud around the mountain tops.

"They call these islands the Ladrones," said Ambrose, with a sneer, "and ladrone is Spanish for 'a robber;' they gave the islands this name because they found the natives confirmed thieves."

"Humph! that reminds me of the niggers," rejoined Tom Hawser, "who are for ever reviling each other as cussed black fellows."

"Robbers!" repeated Ambrose, sternly. "Aye, and where will you find in all the universe such ruthless thieves and tyrants as these same Spanish bigots, who have carried fire and sword into the fairest regions of the earth, and have swept off whole races of the harmless and peaceful inhabitants? And where are these proud, vengeful Dons now? Their haughty assumption is as ridiculous as the strut of a peacock. Ah! mate, there is retribution even in this world! Conscience may sleep, but it never dies; justice may linger, but it strikes at last."

"Belay all that," grunted Tom, "you put me into the doldrums."

For a moment the pirate stood with his arms folded and his eyes cast down as in deep thought; then he said, with a hollow laugh,

"You are right, my hearty; it will not do to brood over deeds that cannot be undone. But I must leave you to watch over the boy, whilst I go in search of the proa in which I sailed to this island; she is hidden under some rocks on yon side of the island. I fear that the Spanish villains have found her."

"Well, as I'm to act as Sawbones, mate, you must tell me what sort o' treatment the patient requires," said Tom.

"Oh, he will give you little trouble," returned Ambrose, with a smile; "he will sleep for some hours. You may from time to time moisten his parched lips with lime-juice and water; your chief care will be to save him from the stings of the plaguy mosquitoes, ticks, centipedes, and other vermin. When he wakes, I trust you will find him calm and rational. Should I not return, do not endanger yourself by going in search of me; you will find plenty of arms and ammunition in the cave, to defend yourselves in case of attack—do not fire a shot if you can help it; there will be no need to do so, for the fowls on the plain are so tame that you can boldly approach them, and both they and the wild cattle are easily run down."

"All right, my hearty," said the boatswain; "trust me for keeping my weather eye open."

"Good bye, Tom, I will return before sunset, or if not, do not wait for me; push on to the extremity of the island, and waylay some of the Indians, who land from their proas, and bribe or frighten them, or do both, but secure a proa, and make all sail for Guajan, where you will find, at least, a Manilla ship. Good bye."

Mark Ambrose waved his hand, threw his carabine across his shoulders, and slowly descended the hill.

Tom Hawser gazed after him for a few moments with a puzzled look, and then gravely shaking his head, turned and made his way back to the cave.

Jack Rushton still lay sunk in profound repose.

Tom Hawser sat down by the boy's side, and employed himself in fanning off the clouds of mosquitoes and other winged tormentors that hovered in clouds about the couch.

He carried out the directions given him by Ambrose with manly tenderness.

From time to time he wetted the boy's parched lips, and bathed his forehead.

After another hour had passed, Jack began to show favourable symptoms.

His breast heaved more lightly; a gentle perspiration suffused his brow, and his features grew tranquil and composed.

The fever fit which had prostrated him had been brought on by the pain of his wound and the terrible excitement through which he had passed, aided by the effects of the tropical heat and malaria.

His young constitution, however, strengthened by hardy exercise and unabused by excesses, was well able to withstand the short and sharp attack.

The good-hearted old seaman watched with pleasure the favourable change in the patient's condition.

For an instant Tom had left Jack's side, and was replenishing the wood fire, when a sudden bark from Snap caused him to turn sharply round.

If he had seen a ghost he could not have looked more startled.

There sat Jack, upright in the bed, staring wonderingly at him, while Snap was fawning upon his young master with joy and affection.

"Am I dreaming or waking?" murmured Jack, faintly, as he raised his hand to his head, and looked at the seaman in great bewilderment. "Surely I am not on board the 'Titania!' and yet you must be Mr. Hawser, our bo'swain."

"Avast! Mr. Rushton," returned the old tar, giving the lad a bearish hug. "Lor bless your peepers, which I thought were battened down for ever, I *was* Tom Hawser, the bo'swain; but what I am now would be harder to say."

"A poor castaway like myself, Mr. Hawser, I suppose," said Jack, sadly.

"Ah!" he gasped, wearily, "what a long, long dream of horror it has been. I have been ill—mad! What did I rave about?"

"Shiver me, Mr. Rushton," said Tom Hawser, dolefully, shaking his head; "but though it's gratifying to a chap's wanity to find that things turns out according to his foreshowing, I must own, as in this case of ourn, it would ha' been better if the sceptical lubbers that jeered me for my warnins had had the laugh of me. We sailed on a Friday, but it must a' been a on-common black Friday, too. Poor Cap'en Transom! a worthier man, or a more thorough seaman, never walked the quarter deck, or mounted the main gangway."

Jack was now sufficiently recovered to sit up and join in conversation, though he still looked very pale and weak.

"But you must tell me how you managed to escape the butcherly scoundrels, Mr. Hawser?" he said.

"Why, blow me, sir, if I can tell ye the rights on't," returned the old boatswain, rubbing his bald pate; "but it fell out summut in this way. You remember when the poor lads — cut down to the last handful — gave up fighting, some leaping overboard, some holding out their throats to be cut by the Malay devilskins — some hauling down the flag and pleading for mercy —you remember when things had arrived at that pint—"

"No, I don't, Mr. Hawser."

"No! Why, my stars, Mr. Rushton, and you fought like a young tiger through the hottest of it."

"But just after the captain fell," explained Jack, "and I was rushing to the main hatch in hopes of saving little Nellie, I got struck down by a blow from a pike or a hatchet, and the last thing that I remember is rolling down the companion ladder; then all is dark, till light dawned upon me— the bright moonshine, which lit up the dusky forms of a hundred sleeping murderers in the Pirates' Lair."

"And how came you into such quarters?"

"I am not quite sure that I can tell you; but by putting this and that together—snatches of conversation I overheard in the cavern," replied Jack, "I believe that after the vessel was taken, Mark Ambrose went aboard her, and seeing me lying senseless, persuaded the chief miscreant, Don Pablo, to take me ashore in one of the proas; but, pray, go on with your own story."

"Well, Mr. Rushton, as I had laid about pretty lustily, I made a clear space around me; and when I saw the villains murdering my onhappy shipmates in cold blood, and yelling and scoffing at their cries for quarter, I crouched down behind the slide of one of the carronades. The pirates were too busy at their hellish work to notice me; they went below and rummaged the cabins and the hold for plunder.

"They laid hands on everything worth removal, and shipped off whatever they selected in the proas and row-boats.

"Then they ran their cursed red flag with its skull and sword up to the masthead; but soon began tumbling over the sides into their boats as fast as they could.

"The proas were busy picking up the

ducks, for ever so many of the villains had been flung, or had fallen, overboard.

"I wondered why they cleared off so suddenly and quickly; but the reason was soon made clear.

"I was well nigh stunned by a terrific explosion forward.

"The magazine had been fired, and, in the twinkle of a hand-pike, the poor 'Titania' was in blazes.

"She careened; her masts, with all their gear, toppled over and went by the board.

"Then she settled slowly down, and was sinking fast.

"There was no time for counting fingers, I assure you.

"Afraid of being dragged down in the eddy made by the sinking vessel, I sprang over the starboard bulwark, and swam for the nearest reef.

"I reached it more dead than alive.

"It was a bare coral rock, and if I had kept on my pins I must have been seen from the schooner, the boats, or the shore.

"Howsomever, I laid down flat on my face, and covered myself as well as I could with the sea-weed.

"In about half-an-hour the pirate sharks had disappeared, and the schooner sheered off a point to the nor'rad, and dropped her anchor.

"It was horrible to see the gashed and bloated bodies of my poor messmates with their fixed, bolting, glassy eyes upturned, as if to call down vengeance, as they floated on the swell, and bounced agen the sides of the reef.

"The tide was rising fast, and at high tide the rock is full a fathom under water.

"I was forced to leave the reef; but not wanting to run into the wolf's mouth, I cast about to find some drifting spar on which I might get away from the pirate's den, and make for the other island.

"I found some sheathing boards and rope yarn that was lashed on to the reef, and lashing 'em together formed a sort of raft, on which I pushed off, and, paddling with a piece of timber, soon made way, for the sea was as smooth as a duck-pond.

"I got off clear.

"Night had come on, and they seemed to be keeping but a dead-man's watch along the cliffs, for jest as I were passing under that tall peak with the palms atop, a face peered over the top of it, and I saw the steel barrel of a long carabine sparkle in the bright moonbeams.

"A voice hailed me from aloft—in English, too; it must a been Mark's—but it warn't likely as I could stop to exchange compliments.

"I paddled away as fast as I could.

"Looking up I saw the fellow on the cliff, with the gun to his shoulder, taking steady aim at me.

"I stood up and pointed aloft to the starry skies.

"The fellow, whoever he was, seemed taken aback, for he lowered his gun, looked at me for a moment, then waved his hand towards the other island, turned, and disappeared behind the trees.

"About six bells I got ashore and I hid myself in the woods."

"And about how long have you been on the island?"

" This is the fourth day, Mr. Rushton.

" My first care upon reaching the land was to look out for some elewated place where I could fit a signal as might attract the notice of the tops-men on some passing ship.

" I mounted the highest hill I could find, and kept a bright look out on all quarters.

" I did not see you land, nor Mark neither, but I saw the pirates cross the narrow strait in their proas and put in shore on the other side of the island.

" I thought they had come in search of me, so I posted myself on a ledge of the rocks where there was one of those queer moniments left by the aborigines, a square pyramid with a stone summut resemblin' half a Dutch cheese stuck at the top; it was just on the verge of the ledge, and by some wolcanic conwulsion of natur', the sandstone at the base on it had given way, and it inclined like that curious old tower I've read on in Spain or Italy.

" The leaning tower of Pisa, perhaps," suggested Jack.

" Aye, maybe; when I were young, Mr. Rushton, I knew all about sich ruins and other nat'ral curiosities.

" I had a old book of geography; but, lor' bless your eyes, sir ! the maps and sea-charts in it were constructed by some land-lubber as knowed no more about navigation than a marine.

" But avast, I'm shifting a-lee. To come back to my tack, Mr. Rushton, I loosened the earth under the bottom of this odd relic of antiquity, intendin' to shove it over on to the heads of the inwaders should they attempt to storm my fortress, and then make a dash at 'em with my cutlass, which I still had with me, and die like a Briton in hot fight—but you're looking deadly pale, Mr. Rushton. I'm tiring you; shall I bring to ?"

" No, no; heave ahead, Mr. Hawser," returned Jack, " but first give me a drink of water from that calabash."

The old boatswain complied with this request.

Jack drank deep, and then leaned languidly back upon his rude couch, and closing his eyes, listened with interest to the boatswain's story.

" I clambered to the top of the hill, and, lying down among the stones, watched the movements of the pirate wretches. I saw them enter a valley, and then lost sight of them, for the hills were high and the woods thick.

" Presently I caught the sound of distant shouts, and every now and then the crack of a gunshot, and I knew that they were in pursuit of some poor castaway like myself."

" It was Mark Ambrose and me they were chasing," rejoined our hero.

" Aye, Mr. Rushton, and well for you that you managed to outsail the raffs— but to finish my long yarn. Towards evening I saw the wood a-fire, and a grand though awful spectacle it were. I heard the yells of the Malay wolves, and I thought they were making for my mountain. I ran down into a dark ravine and hid myself till the alarm had passed over, and then I crept forth, and, strolling among the hills, dropped in upon my old messmate Ambrose and yourself in this cave."

"And where is Ambrose now?" asked Jack.

"He has gone to the other side of the island to look for the proa, and to bring away some stores and ammunition."

At this moment Snap, who had been lying upon the couch, sprang to the ground, and running to the entrance, gave a loud, sharp bark.

Then he crouched back with a surly growl, and returned to the side of his young master.

A heavy step was heard.

The dark form of Ambrose appeared at the entrance.

He carried a cask on his shoulder and a canvas bag in his hand.

He flung these down and stepped to the couch.

"What cheer, lad?" he asked kindly, taking our hero's hand and laying his finger on the wrist.

"I thank you, my dear friend Mark," said the boy, with a pleasant smile. "You are an excellent medico. I am almost well now."

"That's hearty!" returned the seaman, "and I bring you good news."

"I am sure it is welcome then," said poor Jack.

"You will see old England yet, lad! I have steered the proa to a creek close by. I escaped being seen by a miracle, for the gang are still on the island. To-morrow we shall sail for San Ignacio."

"But why not to-night?"

"It would not be safe; the schooner lies abreast of the island. I know by her signals that Don Pablo and the rest have been summoned to go aboard, maybe to overhaul another prize. Besides, I am weary, and as hungry as a starved jackal."

With this he seated himself before the fire, still keeping his eyes constantly fixed upon the boy.

Tom Hawser bestirred himself, and a fowl being cooked, the three made a hearty meal.

Then Ambrose stretched himself before the blaze, and bidding Tom mount guard for an hour or two, fell into a deep sleep.

CHAPTER XIX.

HAND TO HAND AND FOOT TO FOOT.

Tom seated himself at the entrance of the cave, and kept a sharp look-out.

Our hero, leaning his head upon his arm, lay quite still, watching the countenance of the sleeping pirate.

The face of the guilty man worked fitfully; now a grim smile rested on his lips, then his sullen brow lowered in a black frown.

He seemed to be buried in a profound, even trance-like slumber, but his repose was not dreamless.

From time to time he muttered in his sleep.

The heat was oppressive, and even the watchful Tom had much ado to keep his eyes open.

Our hero, however, was broad awake, and he listened to the deep breathing of the pirate and the incessant droning buzz of insects, and the various sounds of animal life that rung through the woods, with a feeling of restlessness and excitement.

Evening was at hand; the long, monotonous hours passed heavily.

Jack felt in no humour for conversation.

His thoughts were busy with strange recollections and vague anticipations of the future.

All at once, Tom Hawser leaped to his feet, with a startled air.

Seeing the wild expression of his face, Jack sprang up on the couch.

"What's in the wind, Mr. Hawser?" he asked, quickly.

"Hist!" cried the seaman, holding up his hand, "some one is hailing from the mountains."

"It is the pirate gang!" cried Jack. "Toss me that firelock; I am so weak I cannot stand. Wake Ambrose."

Snap now sprang to the door and uttered a fierce growl.

The cavern was situated in the side of a rocky bank.

A distant shout.

A long crackle as of musketry!

Ambrose started from his sleep.

"We are beset," cried Jack; "let us die like heroes, Mark; kill that villain Pablo if you can."

The seaman scowled fiercely; then with a stolid air he took up a carabine, and walked to the entrance of the cave.

Jack got off the couch.

He staggered forwards, trailing a gun in his hand.

His limbs tottered, not with fear, but weakness, and he was fain to rest himself against the rocks.

A yell was heard.

Then the swift scampering of flying feet.

A man came bounding like a hunted deer down the side of the rocky bank, and, by a tremendous spring, reached the ground just beside Tom Hawser.

He sank on one knee.

In his arms he clasped a little girl. His clothes were torn, and his black, haggard face looked fearfully behind him.

It was the negro Pompey.

Jack and Tom Hawser gave a shout of amazement.

"Why, strike my old hulk, if it ain't Uncle Pomp, the cap'en's walet!" cried Tom. "And little Miss Nell, too! Speak, man, where are the villains?" and he grasped his fire-arms with ferocious purpose.

"Oh laws! oh golly! Mass' Hawser, if yo be him for troof, not him duppy (ghost), de cuss pirate, de—" here he stopped, panting for breath, "dey'se close down. Oh, jumbo, sar! dey'se killed dis child slick dead; nebber can run no one step mo', sar, not to save lilly missee se'f. O, I dead—I killed outright!"

And he sank back in a convulsion of fatigue and agitation.

"Bring them into the cave," said Ambrose, quickly. "The pirates may pass us without finding our hiding-place. Ha, here they come!"

With a shout, three hideous-looking ruffians burst from the trees.

They rushed down the rocks.

Brandishing their weapons, and whooping like savages, they sped towards the gallant little band.

Ambrose, Tom, and our hero presented their fire-arms.

The hunted castaways were at bay.

There was a long and ominous pause, the pirates slinking back irresolute—for an instant repulsed by the desperate and determined aspect of their brave opponents. No one stirred; each kept his foot advanced, and his weapon levelled, as if pausing on the verge of the crisis which was to decide his individual fate for life or for death.

At length a shout from the woods seemed to revive the sinking courage in the breasts of the assailants of the little band of castaways.

One of them drew trigger.

His clumsy firelock only flashed in the pan.

Ambrose was upon him in an instant, and the struggle was fierce. An ugly Malay ruffian attacked Tom Hawser with his creese; but the sturdy boatswain, winding his arm round the fellow's supple waist, hurled him off to a great distance, dashing his head against the rocky wall.

The third pirate, a savage, whose face was tattooed and painted in a revolting style, fired his musketoon, and then turned on his heel and fled like a hare.

"The mongrel curs!" growled Tom Hawser. "Why, look how the lubbers are clapping on all sail, and scudding afore the wind as if a whole ship's crew of 'jollies' were in full chase."

"Aye, messmate," returned Ambrose, quietly; "but these are but the jackals that run before the lion. Look yonder."

"Aye, shiver me, that's the skipper himself!" cried Tom, in dismay. "And considering he's but a Spanish swab, he's a smart chap; but, strike my topsails, if he comes athwart hawse with me, I'll play old Harry with his figure-head."

"Away!" cried Ambrose, sternly. "Take up the child; the negro is exhausted. Come, Jack. What! Cheerly, lad, are ye so pale? I thought the sight of the cursed pirates would have brought back the colour to your cheeks. We'll beat 'em yet, Jack."

"Aye," groaned our hero; "but I am disabled. But I will have one blaze at the villains. Give me your pistol."

CHAPTER XX.

A TERRIBLE CRISIS.

Jack Rushton with trembling hand fired his pistol at the advancing pirates.

He was too much shaken by the effects of his late attack of fever to be able to take steady aim, and the bullet from his pistol flew over the head of Don Pablo, doing no further damage than cracking one of the low, weeping branches of the trees.

Ambrose grasped the lad in his arms,

and would have lifted him from the ground, and carried him away bodily; but the brave boy resisted this intention, and taking firm hold of his defender's hand, stumbled along by his side.

Tom Hawser had placed the child on his shoulder.

Her pale, soft cheek pressed against his crisp, dark hair, and her dimply arm drooped listlessly round his neck, for she had swooned from fatigue and fright.

As for poor Pomp, he looked a picture of distress.

His clothes fluttered in tatters, his limbs quivered, his face was bathed in perspiration, his thick lips were parted wide, and his breath came short and thick, while his bloodshot eyes rolled in their sockets with a glare of horror and despair.

He had much ado to keep pace with his companions, who were threading the maze of banks, trees, and rocks with the speed of lightning.

However, he did his best, and though he staggered in his walk, and from time to time brought his woolly pate in sharp concussion against rocks and branches, blundered on in some fashion, and kept pretty close in the rear of his fellow fugitives.

"Ombre de Dios! you have let them escape!" raved Don Pablo, stamping his foot, in a towering rage, as he rushed to the side of one of the pirates whom Ambrose had felled, and who was rising painfully, his hand to his wounded head.

"Maria purissima!" groaned the pirate; "what could I do, senor? The foul fiend protects the vile heretics."

Don Pablo gave a grunt, expressive of his disgust, and then nimbly scrambled on to the top of a steep bank.

He stood in a graceful attitude, with his left hand shading the light of the rising sun from his eyes, while in his right he grasped a musket.

"Alfuera!" he shouted. "After them, you dastards! They are making for yonder cleft in the rocks, where they may hold out against us for hours. There goes the traitor Ambrose. Tira! fire at him!"

Several of the pirates in the valley below obeyed this mandate by discharging their pieces at their late comrade; but the seaman was rushing so swiftly among the mazes of the trees and rocks that they failed to hit him.

Don Pablo scrambled yet higher and higher from one boulder to another up the mountain side.

He looked steadily for a moment in the direction by which the fugitives were winding upwards through the thickset trees.

He could track their progress by the rustling of the boughs and underwood; but their bodies were concealed by the thick foliage.

At length the head of poor little Nellie, perched on Tom Hawser's shoulder, appeared through an opening in the wood.

A sneer curled the pirate's lips.

He half raised the musket.

A pang of conscience caused even that ruthless miscreant to pause for a moment.

However, the hesitation was but momentary. Growling a savage execration, the scoundrel aimed at the child, and fired!

But he had miscalculated his distance; for, though he had taken sure aim, he failed to reach his mark, which was beyond the range of the bad piece which he had snatched from the hands of one of his attendants.

With an impatient exclamation, he flung the musket away, and, drawing a long pistol from his sash, crouched along like a crawling panther, watching for another chance to destroy his victims.

Meantime, Ambrose and the rest of the little band had reached the cleft in the mountain to which the pirate chief had alluded. Here they halted.

Aided by Tom and Pomp, Mark Ambrose rolled a large stone across the entrance of the narrow passage, and behind this breast-work they all cowered down, a perfect hailstorm of bullets rattling over their heads.

The place in which they had ensconced themselves was certainly a post of vantage, for it was impossible to reach it from below, except by a narrow, rugged, winding way, in which two persons could not walk abreast.

" Hark ye, messmates," said Ambrose, when they were settled down under the rough shelter of the mass of stone, " I will defend this post till the last, but you must escape. Tom, do you look to the child; and you, lad, give me a parting grip and begone! You see that narrow path through the bushes; it will lead you to the verge of a precipice, down which you may scramble at the risk of your necks, maybe, but if you can escape the peril of the descent you will stand a fair chance of getting clear

away from the pursuit. Keep under the shadow of the rocks till you come to the shore, and there hide among the caverns, and keep a bright look out for a sail. If I do not come to you, conclude that I have been killed by these devils. Don't linger an instant— away!"

" Never, Mark," returned our hero, clasping his arm. " Whatever your faults or crimes, you have proved a staunch friend to me; I would rather perish with you than leave you alone in danger."

" God bless ye, lad! God bless ye!" returned the seaman, with genuine emotion, as he wrung the boy's hand; "but I have no other wish in life but to save ye. Better I should be shot down by my fellow rascals than be swung off at the yardarm on a king's ship. Only get away, and I shall be satisfied: if you are taken, my labour is all lost, and death will be bitter indeed—and, Jack, mind your promise, never let *her* know that I turned a black pirate. I have spoken to Tom, and he will keep the secret. That's all I have to say, lad; and now, good-bye."

" Never, never, never!" cried our hero, fervently. " They shall not hang you, Mark, I will plead for you on my knees, so will Tom, so will dear little Nellie. You will be pardoned, and will live yet for happiness."

" Live!" cried the pirate with a scowl. " You are obstinate, and would rob me of my only solace. Jack, for your mother's sake, think only of saving yourself. You can do me no good— your presence unmans me; besides, there is the child to save!"

"INEZ STRUCK THE PISTOL UPWARDS, WHICH EXPLODED IN THE AIR."

" But why can't you come with us ?"

" Then, who is to defend this pass ? No, let me stay till you have got clear off. I give you my word that I will follow you; let that content ye, lad. And now, away ! "

As he spoke, a bullet whistled past his head.

He cowered down.

" Hark ye, Jack," gasped the pirate, through his clenched teeth ; " never a lily-livered shoresman, in his first gale, feels more coward-like than I do, *while you are here*. Drag this mad fool away, Tom, if you would save his life and the child's."

Tom Hawser, conscious of the utter futility of arguing further with a man of such a stern and determined character, hastily caught our hero by the arm and hurried him away.

Sheltering himself from the volley of bullets which were fired at him by the ruffians below, Mark Ambrose lay under the beetling crag, and watched the little party as they rushed along their narrow and stony path.

They had not proceeded far before our hero began to show signs of exhaustion, and though he made a brave effort to keep pace with Tom and the negro, was evidently much distressed.

Seeing this, the old sailor resigned little Nellie to the faithful negro, and, winding his arm round the poor boy's waist, hurried him onwards.

During this, Mark Ambrose was bravely defending his post by firing his pistols at the invaders, and hurling down huge stones upon their heads.

Pompey, who had recovered his breath, placed the child upon his shoulder, and sprang away at a gallant rate.

He leaped from bank to bank, with the agility of a deer, and being fleeter of foot than his companions, soon distanced them, and disappeared in the intricacies of the wood.

Tom Hawser had no sooner lost sight of the negro and the child, than he was alarmed by hearing a loud shout behind him.

Turning sharply round, he beheld Ambrose fiercely struggling with an overwhelming crowd of the pirates.

Yet amidst the desperate struggle the unfortunate man seemed to be influenced only by one thought, which was his intense desire that Jack should escape.

He waved his hand, and pointed to a narrow defile between the hills through which the fugitives might make their way to the sea-shore.

" Let us go back, Mr. Hawser," cried Jack, nerving himself to exertion, though his limbs tottered as if he were smitten with palsy, while his brain seemed a-fire. " Do not let the villains butcher him before our eyes; let us make one effort to save him."

" Belay ! " growled the boatswain. " It's no us eat all, Mr. Rushton. What can we do agin such odds ? Let us save the poor cap'en's child ! "

But the loud despairing yell that resounded from the woods proclaimed the terrible truth that Pomp and Nellie had also fallen into the hands of their murderous foes.

Making their way to the top of a high bank covered with stately breadfruit trees, they looked down into the narrow defile which Ambrose had indicated by such frantic gesticulations.

Pompey and the little girl were descried surrounded by the pirates, who had secured the negro's arms, and had dragged Nellie from his grasp.

Maddened at the scene, Tom Hawser levelled his musket at the villains, and fired.

One of them was evidently struck, for he staggered back, and dropped upon his knees.

With a yell of fury, the others, who had caught sight of Tom and our hero, rushed up the mountain side.

Jack would have made one desperate charge upon the advancing assailants, but Tom drew him backwards.

"Let us escape if we can, Mr. Rushton," said he, in a hoarse and trembling voice. "While there's life there's hope, my hearty. It is plain that the sharks will not injure their prisoners without the sanction of the skipper. If we can escape we may live to do our mates good service; if we are killed, there's an end of their chance as well as ours. Don't let's haul down our flag till we have done our best to outsail the enemy."

CHAPTER XXI.

ON BOARD THE PIRATE SCHOONER.

BREATHLESS, and flushed from his late fierce and protracted struggle, Mark Ambrose stood passively, surrounded by his wild, ferocious-looking captors.

He had given up the contest, and seemed utterly unconscious of his own terrible position and absorbed in his intense anxiety on account of his flying comrades.

With strained eyes, and hands tightly clasped, he watched the old seaman, as, half dragging, half supporting Jack Rushton, he dashed up the mountain, hotly chased by the pirates, who from time to time discharged their fire-arms at the fugitives.

He beheld them pass over the brow of the hill and disappear, their pursuers being a long distance in the rear.

A faint smile stole across his stern, manly face, and he turned round and glanced at his captors with a look of apathy and indifference.

Now that the excitement of the chase and the final struggle was over, the pirates seemed less jubilant at having captured their prey than might, under the circumstances, have been expected.

But the fact was, that they felt some amount of awe at the anticipation of the terrible scene that was likely to ensue, for they well knew that their fiendish leader would wreak terrible vengeance upon the rebel who had set his authority at defiance, and had given him so much trouble.

Besides, there were not wanting many of the gang who were well disposed towards their late officer, for he had often stood between them and the violence of the tyrant, and the desperate resistance he had made tended rather to impress the murderous rascals favourably than otherwise, for they could not but feel some admiration for a man who had shown such indomitable pluck and resolution.

They stood regarding him grimly but half abashed.

One or two, however, overcoming their remorseful hesitation, advanced towards him, and pointed to his cutlass and pistols.

With the haughty resignation and taciturnity of a defeated Indian brave, Mark Ambrose took the weapons from his side and calmly handed them over to the men.

"I am at your mercy, comeradoes," he said, with a half sneer. "Slaves as ye are, you have bowed your necks under the heel of your despotic master, and will all in turn suffer the same fate as that which I know awaits me. If there were a man among ye, he would stand to my side, and defy the tyrant whose power rests solely on your craven submission."

The men lowered their glances, or exchanged significant looks.

"Santa Maria!" cried one of them, with a nervous start; "do not listen to the traitor. Look, look, here the senor comes."

With a dignified stride, and a subtle, malignant smile lighting up his evil countenance, the pirate chief advanced, followed by a train of his myrmidons.

"So, Master Ambrose," he said, speaking in English, and with a deep tone of vindictive gratification, "the game is up, eh? you surrender at discretion."

"I have achieved my purpose, senor," returned Ambrose, with undaunted calmness. "I have rescued the boy from your cruel hands; he will gain the shore, where a flying proa is hidden, in which he may escape to San Ignacio; and, moreover, I shall die with the satisfaction that my death will be speedily avenged."

"By whom, my desperado?" sneered the pirate.

"Look to yourself, Don Pablo," returned Ambrose, with a chuckle of quiet triumph. "An English frigate of war lies off yonder bluff."

"Es varded, senor," rejoined one of the pirates, in a breathless tone. He had just returned from the pursuit of Tom Hawser and our hero. "'Tis true; we sighted her from the top of the hill."

The pirate chief turned white with rage, and gnashed his teeth.

He quivered with the strong effort it demanded to subdue the impulse which prompted him to kill his victim upon the spot.

"Muy ben," he said, with affected carelessness, though it was evident the unexpected intelligence had made a deep impression upon him. "We know how to take care of ourselves, how to conquer foes, and to punish traitors. You have violated your oath, betrayed the band, defied my authority, and you shall die by no easy death, believe me, for, as your treason is outrageous, your punishment shall be terrible."

"Do your worst, villain," returned the stoic Englishman, with quelling sternness; "but if you would not degrade yourself in the eyes of these, your cringing slaves, forbear your threats of cowardly cruelty, which would better become a weak, vindictive woman than a haughty hidalgo who boasts of his high descent. Bah! What is your cat-like courage, thief and murderer, but the desperation of a felon, justly doomed to the gallows."

"Malraya!" thundered the Don, beside himself with passion, as he dashed down his pistol. "Do not think to provoke me to slay you now; I will make you change your tone, English dog, if there be any virtue in fire and steel. Bind the traitor, and drag him away to the boats."

Ambrose was immediately set upon by the subordinate ruffians, and pinioned with ropes.

A noose was flung round his neck, and he was hauled furiously along, for Pablo, beginning to feel apprehensive that some of the men-of-wars' men might have landed on the island, was anxious to get afloat.

They reached the shore.

The proas were already launched, and lay on the heaving bosom of the sea, with their quaint cocoa-matting sails half unfurled.

Near them were gathered a group of pirates, awaiting the arrival of their chief and surrounding their prisoners— poor Pomp and his pretty little charge.

The negro was evidently a prey to the most horrible fear, for he quivered in every limb, and his eyes rolled wildly from side to side.

Dragged ignominiously by the neck, Ambrose was brought to the spot.

Don Pablo followed him, and marked his degradation with a satanic leer.

"Kill the negro," said the pirate chief, coolly.

Pomp, though he could not understand Spanish, yet easily divined the meaning of the pirate chief's significant gesture, and sank upon his knees.

One of the pirates drew his creese.

At this moment a proa was seen sailing round a headland, and a lady appeared in the outrigger, waving a scarf.

"Maldito!" growled the pirate; "it is Inez. The mad woman will be our destruction. Get the prisoners into the boat, and take them aboard the schooner; I will stay to receive the senorita."

"But this black fellow, senor?" said one of the Malays, clapping the edge of his dreadful dagger to poor Pomp's throat.

"Not before her eyes, you dog. Away with them; I will follow you."

Ambrose, Pomp, and the child were hurried into one of the proas, the sail was unfurled, and the curiously-constructed vessel soared away before the freshening breeze.

Crossing the strait that divided the two islands, the proa coasted the Pirates' Lair, and putting into a little creek, was soon alongside of the dark hull of the schooner.

The prisoners were taken aboard.

They were immediately conducted to the lower decks. Nellie was separated from Pomp and Ambrose, who were brutally thrust into the hold, while the child was confined in one of the cabins.

Shortly after Don Pablo and his wife came aboard.

The pirate chief seemed in evil mood.

As soon as he had reached the deck he sprang upon the main gangway, and, taking up a glass, scanned the horizon anxiously.

"Aloft, there !" he shouted to the men in the tops.

"Si, senor," answered the fellows.

"Is the frigate still in sight ?"

"No, senor ; she got under weigh about an hour ago, and steered for Sanpan."

"Good," he murmured, his brow clearing.

Then he descended amidships, and said curtly,

"Weigh anchor; if a sail appears let me be called. Come, Inez, we will go below."

All was bustle on deck.

The hands aloft were busy in making sail, while those on board worked hard at the windlass.

There was some confusion, much cursing and swearing, and the work was performed in a hurried and slovenly manner by the undisciplined horde ; not that they were bad sailors, but in such lawless association the quiet promptitude and perfect order of the legitimate service is not to be obtained even by the most skilful and determined ring-leader.

The schooner was nevertheless a splendid craft, and a clipping sailer, and as she flew along before the freshening gale the motley crew laughed and cheered with much spirit.

But soon there was a dead hush, as, with cloudy brow and the aspect of a sulky lion prowling forth from his den, Don Pablo came from the after hatchway and walked forward.

"Bring the prisoners on deck," he said.

A number of the ruffians rushed off to obey this order.

In a few moments Ambrose, Nellie, and the negro were brought on deck.

"Fools !" snarled the chief, impatiently, "I did not want you to bring the child !"

"Pardon, senor," said one of the men, humbly, as he took the affrighted little one by the hand, and was about to lead her away.

"Hold—let her remain !" said Don Pablo, thoughtfully.

Ambrose stood with folded arms and an air of impassable fortitude, guarded on either side by the savage miscreants.

The pirate captain, nervously twitching his moustache and darkly frowning, paced moodily up and down.

At length he stopped, and fixed a stern glance upon Ambrose.

"You have expressed an opinion that the frigate we sighted this morning is in chase of us," he said. "What reason have you for supposing that to be the case ?"

Ambrose smiled.

"Because she is evidently cruising about the islands, and has twice appeared off the same point," he answered, quietly ; "and you may have heard from the senora that there has been a stir made at Manilla, and that the captain of an English vessel on the cruise for slavers and Japanese pirates has undertaken the task of chastising the audacious gang who have dared to attack an English vessel—but, avast! what is this to me?" he added, shrugging his broad shoulders and turning quietly aside, "I have no interest now in common with you or your band, Don Pablo. I served you faithfully; you promised to save the boy, and you did not keep your word; you threatened my life; it was you who broke faith, not I. Enough! do what you will with me; I am in your power, and I neither ask nor wish for mercy!"

"Nor deserve it," growled the pirate, who was evidently disconcerted at the intelligence he had heard; "but tell me, Ambrose, did you make out the frigate's colours?"

"Aye," returned the seaman, smiling grimly, "the bunting that streamed at her peak was—the Union Jack of Old England!"

"Maria purissima!" gasped the pirates, with a general start.

"Then she must be the same vessel of which Donna Inez spoke," said the chief. "Pedrillo, there!"

"Si, senor," answered the youth, stepping up adroitly.

"Did you hear the name of the English captain?"

"Si, senor," returned the lad. "His name is Captain Varney; and the ship he commands is called the 'Fearless.'"

His cheek waning ashy pale, and his brow lowering darkly, Ambrose started back at such an unexpected announcement.

"This Captain Varney, senor, is an elderly man," continued Pedrillo, with a smile; "but he has the most beautiful young wife in the world. Her health is delicate, and she sailed with her husband, the physician having recommended her to take a sea voyage. I saw the Senora Inglesa at Manilla, where her husband left her when he received his dispatches."

Mark Ambrose quivered in every limb, and leaned heavily against the bulwarks.

Don Pablo laughed jeeringly.

"And so, amigo," said he, "you will lose your revenge."

"Aye, senor," returned Ambrose, in a hoarse whisper, and with an air of strange dejection.

The pirate watched his prisoner keenly.

A thoughtful shade passed over the Spaniard's face.

"It is your own fault, comerado," he said, at length. "You have not done wisely to quarrel with me. But come, you are a good seaman, for once I will pardon, as I love revenge, it is sweet. Revenge? Diable! if a man does me a service I am bound to requite it; if he injuries me—what then? Next to gratifying my own desire for vengeance it pleases me to aid another in wreaking his."

"You are right, senor," cried Ambrose, quickly. "But yet, let vengeance for such an injury as mine——"

He paused, while his cheek burned with confusion that he should trench upon a subject so sacred in such a presence—that he should feel anything but cold scorn and haughty disgust for the accursed, perfidious woman he hated and loved.

Don Pablo watched the working of his dark, expressive face, and at length spoke.

"Listen, Ambrose. If you will take the command of the proas, and follow my directions implicitly, we can save ourselves from these English braggarts. I have conceived a plot by which we may trail them to their destruction. Speak! Will you rejoin our band?"

Ambrose pondered for some time.

A shudder convulsed his frame.

At length he seemed determined to have come to an irrevocable decision, for he lifted his head, and, in a calm and steady voice, replied,

"No, senor; I have forgiven this wrong. I forfeited every claim to vengeance when I joined your pirate crew. I will never again own allegiance to you."

"Muy ben!" I am answered," returned the pirate, with a satanic leer.

He drew a pistol from his belt, and levelled it at the head of Mark Ambrose.

A wild shriek ran along the deck.

Inez, rushing from the main hatch, flung herself into her husband's arms, striking the pistol upwards, which exploded in the air.

The pirate chief attempted to break away from his wife's fervent embrace; but she held him fast, entwining her soft arms about his neck, and pillowing her head upon his shoulder.

"Pablo, my husband," she murmured fondly, "when was the time you could refuse to listen to the entreaties of your own loved Inez? It is but a *small* boon I ask of you—grant this man his life, for *my* sake. Remember, but for him I should never have been restored to you—should have pined till death within the grim walls of my convent dungeon.

Who but he, heretic though he may be called, would have dared the curse of our holy Church? Your most zealous and faithful followers shrunk from the task of snatching a veiled nun from the sanctuary. To him we owe our reunion, love. Well, then, pardon one act of rebellion, for the sake of his many past services; let him go—accept his promise not to betray you, and set him at liberty. You will, Pablo, for my sake?"

This appeal was made in tones so sweet and so endearing as to seem irresistible.

And though by no means to be moved from his ultimate purpose, the villain was somewhat cooled by the soft, imploring accents of this beautiful and devoted girl. He remained silent for some moments.

"Malditi!" he muttered, in a tone of suppressed rage and mortification, as, disengaging himself from her clasp, he paced moodily backwards and forwards, scowling and gnawing his lip. "Woman, you are mad. You know not what you ask. Do you prefer the justly forfeited life of this cursed English traitor and spy, to the lives of myself and the band, which are imperilled by his existence?"

"Keep him a prisoner, then," urged Inez, "but spare his life."

"Muy ben," gasped Don Pablo, gulping down his passion. "What is delayed is not therefore abandoned. I will give him a chance; let him beware how he throws it away, for I swear by the Virgin, that if he remains obstinate he shall die. And now leave me, Inez, I am busy. We are pursued by this rogue's countrymen, who would have no mercy on us if all the saints and angels came down to plead for us. Get you below, Inez; this is no place for you. Do not make me curse the hour when, despite my expressed command, you quitted Manilla. Leave me!"

"But you have promised to grant my request. You will not kill him, Pablo," she said, entreatingly. "You promise that!"

"Si, si," returned her husband, impatiently. "He is undeserving of such clemency, but I will respite him till to-morrow. Be content, and go below, for I am in no mood for further thwarting."

Inez turned away, as if deeply hurt by his harsh and chill repulse, and, with downcast looks, turned humbly from him and went below.

Don Pablo's eyes followed her with a sullen glare.

"Umbre de Dios!" he growled, passionately stamping his foot; "am I turned fool or child? What does the cursed, puling woman here?"

Then, once more turning a ferocious look upon his prisoner, he fingered the hilt of his sabre.

"To-morrow!" he hissed between his clenched teeth.

Then he pointed to the main hatch.

"Take him below," he said to his followers. "Put him in irons, and lash him to the gun that is nearest to my own cabin."

"And the negro, senor, and the child?" asked several of the scoundrels, touching their weapons, and evidently eager for mischief.

"Let the negro be confined in the hold; I have not yet determined how to dispose of him," returned the chief. "As for the child, I leave her in your charge, Sancho, and if you value your life, keep her out of the way of the senora."

These orders were immediately obeyed.

Don Pablo gave orders that the ship should be put about, and run into a narrow creek that penetrated deep through the palmy groves of the island.

CHAPTER XXII.

A BOLD STROKE FOR LIFE AND LIBERTY.

AMBROSE, with Pomp and the negro, had been dragged below, and the pirate chief resumed his restless pacings along the silent deck.

At length, he halted in his angry march, and tossing a large Panama sombrero over his black showering love-locks, leaned against the bulwarks and glanced thoughtfully at the island.

The crew seemed awed by their chief's sullen demeanour, and took good care not to cross the lion's path.

"Lower the quarter-boat," said Don Pablo, suddenly.

A knot of fellows gathered round the capstan started alertly, but rather surprised, at this unexpected order.

However, with them, to hear was to

obey; the davits were manned in an instant, and the boat lowered.

Don Pablo selected a dozen of his smartest men, and rowed ashore.

"The escaped prisoners must be captured," he said, sternly; "they are still on the island, there can be little doubt of that. We must secure them at once, while the coast is clear. There is no time to be lost."

The pirates murmured assent.

"Let us separate into three parties," rejoined the pirate chief; "Balthazar can take the command of one, and explore this side of the island, while I and my party take the other; as for you, Pedrillo, remain here with the rest, and keep a bright look-out. If anything of importance occurs—that is, if you sight the frigate or lay hands on the fugitives —fire your guns as a signal, and we will join you as soon as possible."

"But the boy, senor, and the Englishman—if we catch them?" said Balthazar.

"Kill them at once!" returned Don Pablo, with imperturbable coolness; "We will have no half measures—the traitor, Mark Ambrose, shall die as soon as I return."

He then picked out those whom he wished to form the two exploring parties, and left Pedrillo and two others to guard the boats.

"Should we not catch the fellows before sunset, we will remain all night upon the island," added the chief. "Pedrillo, station yourself upon yonder hill, and maintain your post as sentinel till we have made a circuit of the coast— vamos!"

He flung his carbine across his arm, and marched off in one direction, while Balthazar and his party took the other.

Meantime, Pedrillo, who, it will be remembered, was a mere lad, walked off to the station assigned to him, and slowly mounted the side of a high hill, humming to himself, as he walked along, some Spanish love ditty. The evening was advancing, and the sun was grandly sinking through a lurid haze.

Pedrillo reached the brow of the rocky ascent, and seating himself upon a cushion of brilliant flowers and herbage, leaned his olive cheek upon his hand, and abstractedly gazed upon the gorgeous landscape mapped out beneath him.

Meanwhile, the two men left in charge of the boats—one a half-naked, tattooed African, the other an infamous-looking Malay—relieved from the presence of their dreaded commander, stretched themselves lazily on the beach and began to smoke.

At the same moment that the two exploring parties separated, the castaways they were hunting lay in ambush within a few yards of them.

Crouching low in the giant grass, Jack Rushton and Tom Hawser were lurking side by side.

"Hist!" whispered our hero, as he caught the pirate chief's last words, and saw Pedrillo move away. "Now is our time."

"Do you understand their lubberly lingo?" asked Tom, in an undertone.

"Si, muy poco—very little," returned Jack, with a smile, as, almost breathless with excitement, he took Tom's hand, and led him up the mountain, keeping close under cover of the bush.

"Now, Mr. Hawser, here's an adventure worthy of the most doughty desperado that ever figured in a three volume romance."

And the dauntless lad rubbed his hands, and chuckled as he spoke.

"My jib, Mr. Rushton, then I'm your man, sir; for, smash me, if I arn't tee-total sick o' this game of hide and seek. You are my superior officer, sir, and I defers to your judgment, and if you were to ax me to board the schooner single-handed, I'd undertake to do it. I'd rather be made shark's meat of at once, than live the life of a hunted fox any more."

"That's well said, my hearty," returned Jack. "Look ye, then, poor Mark has risked his life to save us; the villains have him in their power. I don't believe they have killed him yet, for the senorita is aboard, and, besides that, Don Pablo will keep him till he finds an opportunity of wreaking his cruelty upon him."

"Don't be too sure o' that, Mr. Rushton."

"Oh, but I feel confident that I am right; besides, I have Don Pablo's own words for it."

"Why, how's that?"

"I heard him say 'the traitor, Mark Ambrose, shall die as soon as I return;' and the inference is that the poor fellow is reserved for slaughter, like a sheep in a pen awaiting the butcher. Ha, ha! This will be a glorious feat, shipmate."

"Why, you don't mean to say, Mr. Rushton, as you think there's the ghost of a chance of our rescuing him?"

"I care for nothing; I am quite reckless of my life!" returned the boy, with fervour. "I was never a coward, I know, and I have a duty to perform which I will not shrink from come what may. It shall be tried, Mr. Hawser; that is, if you tell the truth when you say you would dare anything rather than live this wretched life any longer."

Tom Hawser shook his head, and touched his forehead.

"I am werry much afeard, Mr. Rushton," said he, "as the Yellow Jack has affected your top hamper."

"If I am mad, you'll find there's method in my madness," returned our hero, buoyantly; "and now for my plan."

"Belay," grunted the old boatswain, "I once heard of a corporal and file o' marines defeatin' the whole imperial army of Chinay; but, split my topmast, if ever——"

"There's nothing impossible to British courage, Mr. Hawser. But, will you listen to what I have to say?"

"In course, Mr. Rushton. Heave ahead, sir; but——"

"Do listen, now; the skipper and all the rest are far away by this time; there's but a dead man's watch kept here; there are but three left in charge of the boats, and they are separated. Now, we are two men."

"Two what? One and a half, you mean," grunted the old salt.

"Thank ye for the compliment," returned Jack, rather fiercely; "I am a *young* man, at least."

"Aye, aye; werry much so, Mr. Rushton," returned the old salt, a merry twinkle in his eye.

"Well," gasped Jack, in great vexation, "if you are twice as big as I,

"THE BOATSWAIN WAS AT WORK IN AN INSTANT, FILING THE PRISONER'S CHAINS."

you ought to have twice as much courage; and, if you had, you would not make much of the odds against us. Look at the sentinel, for instance, a ———"

"Young man."

"Somewhere about my own age," returned Jack, reddening. "And as for those drones yonder, what are the lazy vagabonds but lubberly blacks, whom we can easily overpower? Why, they are half asleep; and, though it's a sneakish expedient, we could creep upon 'em and knock them on the head; then we could seize the boats———"

"And what then, Mr. Rushton?"

"I will show you what can be done then," said Jack, breathlessly. "But first say whether you are willing to help me to overmaster the wretches? At least, it will be something done if we can secure the boats; we can scuttle and sink one of them, and get off in the other."

"Well, that sounds reasonable," said Tom, though in a dubious tone; "but as I used to say to our sailing master— a philosopical, astronomical, book-larnt, self-conceited swab as he was, Mr. Rushton—'theory's one thing, Mr. Gaff,' says I, 'but practice is another.'"

"Well, Mr. Hawser," exclaimed Jack, with a sigh of disappointment; "I did think you were true blue."

"Aye, aye, sir; but not quite green neither," returned the boatswain; "while we are settling the youngster aloft there, the two rascals below will take the alarm, and then what will become of us?"

"We can gag and bind the young fellow first; his position is concealed from those on the beach, and then we

can attend to the others; it only wants care and caution. Follow me."

"Aye, aye, sir," returned the boatswain, with alacrity; for he began to think that in their desperate extremity the wildest scheme might be feasible.

"Here, then," whispered Jack, quickly, as he took a kerchief from his neck, and tied a stone in it. "You see he is sitting on that piece of rock; I will crawl close to him; at the same moment that I fling this round his neck, or clap it into his mouth, do you pop a pistol to his head and threaten to blow his brains out if he stirs hand or foot."

Tom Hawser smiled grimly and nodded, as he drew his heavy pistol from his belt.

Snap, who seemed to understand perfectly what was going on, kept close to his young master's side.

Meanwhile, the unconscious Pedrillo was gracefully reclining against the rock, above the top of which his head appeared, his rich curls streaming in the stealing breeze which blew freshly from the open main.

Jack crawled up the steep bank on his hands and knees.

He held his breath, and his limbs quivered with excitement and suspense.

A bright flush dyed his cheek, called up, no doubt, by a feeling of distaste for the sneakish, garotting, un-English-like expedient necessity had forced upon him.

Tom Hawser was less scrupulous, and a fierce light gleamed in his deep-set grey eyes, and he kept a vicious grip upon his pistol.

They performed the ascent as noiselessly as a pair of Red Indian braves, and in a few seconds were crouching behind the rock.

Jack clenched his teeth, screwed up his courage, and very deliberately looping the handkerchief, flung it over the young Spaniard's head.

Pedrillo, startled out of his senses, opened his mouth to utter a cry of alarm, when the stone clashed in between his teeth and he felt himself struggling in the pangs of strangulation.

At the same moment Tom Hawser rushed round the corner of the rock and clapped the cold steel muzzle of the pistol to the youth's head.

Snap crouched at the captive's feet with a menacing growl.

"One word, and you are a dead man," muttered Tom, sternly.

Jack tied the handkerchief tightly round the lad's head.

Then, seizing his arms, he pulled them backwards over the rock.

Pedrillo seemed so taken by surprise that he offered very little resistance, although he was so nicely caught that the strongest effort would have availed him nothing.

Jack and Tom bound him hand and foot and laid him in a heap, helpless, motionless, and powerless of speech, under the broad leaves of a large plant.

Having thus disposed of Pedrillo, our two adventurers moved away from the spot, and stood staring at each other with blank faces, as if amazed at the ease, quickness, and quietness with which the bold deed had been effected, and mutually turned their eyes upon the dark heap that lay quivering among the luxuriant herbage, as though they could scarcely believe the evidence of their senses.

"Oh, murder! Mr. Rushton," gasped the boatswain, swabbing his smooth, bald pate. "Here's a queer start with a vengeance! How d'ye feel arter that, sir?"

"As if I had just joined a band of Thugs, and had sacrificed my first victim to Bowhanee," returned Jack, drawing a deep sigh. "But I hope we have not killed the poor chap."

"Killed him, boah! only put his jawing tackle out o' gear for awhile. That might a killed a woman, bless her; but he shouldn't be singin' and whistlin' on sentry; sarves him right, the lubber."

"Do you think he can breathe?" asked Jack, taking a step towards the disabled man. "I'll loosen the handkerchief."

"Avast! Never pick up a crushed hornet," returned Tom, catching his arm.

"But see, I've removed his sting," said Jack, showing a long gleaming stiletto.

"Aye, sir, and stopped his buzzing," returned Tom, with a grin. "And now we must wait upon the two ebonies."

"That will be a ticklish job," said Jack.

"I'll tickle 'em, yer honour," growled Tom, clubbing his pistol. "All's fair in war, ye see, and, as we're fighting agin such 'nation long odds, we mustn't be scrupulous. I'll tackle the nigger; you look to the Malay; slice him like a pumpkin if he gives you any trouble."

"Oh, Tom, beware of bloodthirstiness."

"Aye, Mr. Rushton; but beware also

of squeamishness—such sarpints are not to be dealt with like manly foes."

"Come on, then," whispered Jack. "The Malay is smoking—opium, I shouldn't wonder; see how dreamily his tigerish eyes are rolling, and how limp his fingers rest on the handle of his creese. As for the other rascal, he's a regular Mumbo Jumbo of ugliness; it makes one shudder to look at him."

"Belay, then, sir; I'll manage 'em both, even if we have to risk a shot."

"No, no," returned our brave mid, eagerly; "we will do the business together. Here, Snap! whist! down, sirrah! Now, are ye ready?"

"Aye, aye, yer honour. Here goes for death or glory!"

Creeping cautiously through the long grass, and then round the corners of the rocks, the two daring fellows came behind the unconscious pirates, who were sluggishly reclining upon a bank of sand and shingle.

The sagacious dog kept quietly by his master's side, with outstretched neck and pricking ears, and creeping like a setter towards the covey.

Tom was just behind the negro, and raised himself upon one arm.

Unable to keep his fascinated gaze from off his companion, Jack lost his presence of mind when he found himself within a few inches of the Malay, and lingered infirm of purpose, the eyes of the African glaring stupidly at him.

"Ay-yha!" yelled the negro, and he was upon his feet in an instant.

But with a bash Tom's pistol-butt descended upon his woolly pate, and he dropped like a stone—as senseless and motionless.

It was a critical moment for Jack.

Startled from his doze, the Malay uttered a frightful cry, and bounded upon the boy.

Jack, however, caught his leg, and pitched him over, sending him crash down upon the shingles, his murderous creese flying out of his hand.

In an instant Snap sprang at the pirate's throat, and with a deep growl pinned him to the ground.

The negro's sconce had proved harder than Tom's pistol-butt, which was shivered to splinters, so the brave tar attacked his enemy bare-handed.

Thrusting aside the dog, he fixed such a vice-like grip upon the throat of the savage that after a few faint struggles the latter succumbed to the pressure of those iron fingers, and fell backwards quite insensible.

Then there was a pause.

Tom's blood was up.

"Let us finish the work, and kill the scoundrels. What mercy did they show to our poor messmates?" growled Tom.

"For shame, Mr. Hawser," said Jack, indignantly. "We are English sailors, and not Spanish bravoes! We'll gag and bind them, but let's give 'em a chance for their lives, that is if they're not dead already."

"Well, I bides by my orders, in course," grunted Tom; "but, shiver me, if I can see why we should spare the catamarans! Howsomever, fetch a rope from the boat, Mr. Rushton."

Jack complied with this request.

The pirates were gagged, and bound hand and foot, and then dragged under cover of the rocks.

For some time the two heroes remained silent, panting for breath and regarding each other with wonder.

"It seems like a dream!" murmured Jack.

"But it looks like reality, sir," grinned the boatswain. "May I be keel-hauled if you don't live to be a hadmiral!"

"And what's to be done now?" asked Jack, though the question was half addressed to himself, for a vague, wild scheme had entered his rash brains, which he had, even after their late miraculous triumph, scarcely the courage to propound to his companion.

"The first thing as we must do is to scuttle one of the boats, and so prevent the rest of the scoundrels from giving chase; and perhaps we can rig up a sail in the other, and steer for another island."

"Aye, that's the plan," said Jack.

He sprang into the boat.

"Thank heaven!" he cried, earnestly. "It would seem that some special providence has thrown in our way every means for escape. Look here, Mr. Hawser."

"Aye, aye, sir," returned the old tar, stepping briskly to his side.

"Here is a hatchet, a saw, and some files—no doubt belonging to the ship's carpenter of yon precious schooner— and here's some sailcloth and a spar; we can now rig up a sail and fly from this nest of scorpions."

But at this juncture their attention was diverted by Snap, who uttered a deep growl, loudening into a furious bark, as the animal rushed breast deep into the surf, and fixed his gaze upon a round, black object that was discerned through the dim twilight, bobbing up and down upon the sylvan waters.

CHAPTER XXIII.

JACK RUSHTON'S SCHEME FOR RESCUING MARK AMBROSE.

"It is a man!" cried Jack, in great astonishment; "he is swimming to shore."

"Then, shiver me, he'll meet with a warm reception," returned Tom, drawing a pistol.

The swimmer was now upon his feet, and wading through the surf.

Tom took a straight aim at him.

He uttered a yell, and bounding upon land sank on his knees, and held up his hand appealingly.

"Huzza! huzza!" shouted Jack, beside himself with joy. "It is old Pomp! He has escaped!"

And the next moment he was hugging the faithful negro.

"Ah, Mass' Rushton, 'top till me get breff, den me tell yo' all 'bout it," gasped Pomp, in answer to the pressing inquiries of his friends. "Me sit down fo' rest a minute, den tell yo' ebbery-ting."

The poor fellow was dripping with

wet, and exhausted from his long swim. After a short pause, he commenced his story.

"When de cuss pirate cotchee me an' little missee dey take me to dere black ship, and bring 'long Mass' Ambrose too, den de 'Panish skipper he come board wid rest ob de rascals; he 'peak to Mass' Ambrose, tell he kill him right off, if 'pose he not be pirate agen no mo; but Mass' Ambrose—berry brave man dat, sar—he 'fuse, he say him rather die dan be slave to sich like, de cuss tyrant. Garramighty! Heart jump hear him talk bold to de buccra tief! Den Don Pablo he go rampagous; he draw pistol, let fly at Mass' Ambrose; de oder gal, dat de Senora Inez—berry purty female she—Yah! nothing but Creole woman she, not much better'n black folk—nebba yo' mind—she 'trike up de pistol, um go off in de air, den she ax de skipper if he not sabe Mass' Ambrose' life till he kill him in de mornin'; he say him do dat, and he grin hijeous. Mass' Ambrose he took below, and dey lash him to gun in de lower deck."

"I told you so, Mr. Hawser," said our hero, triumphantly; "he is alive—I was sure of it. Go on, Pompey."

"Iss, sar. Me was took below, and lilly missee sep'rate from me—I put in de hold, cober wid chains—Yah! me tink me dead man, but de black cook-mate he come bring me someting to eat, I recompense him directly."

"How, Pomp?" asked Jack.

"Yah; recompense him by him white wool and him tick lip—soch reg'lar nigger he."

"Oh! recognise him."

"Iss, sar, I recognise him, fo' he my ole mate, Casc; serbe wid him 'board ob de Nymp—West Ind'man, sar; he berry sorry see me pris'ner, and aft' mosh palaver, he gib me file; me get out ob irons and creep up de orlop deck, den me jump tro' de port and swim 'shore; dat all I got tell yo."

"But where is Nellie?"

The poor, simple fellow burst into tears, and sobbed like a child.

"'Bliged leab her behind, massa," he moaned, wringing his hands. "Fo' why? p'r'aps now me find chance sabe her; if me tay, no able do noting at all. Oh! massa, me grad to die to sabe she, poor lilly missee; de cuss pirate hab her fast now; most sorry dat dis black rascal leab de cuss ship, raaly so, massa," he added, with another burst of child-like tears.

"Yo look heah, massa," he continued, suddenly brightening up; "dat cruel buccaneer cuss, he on shore now; me wait for he. Lend pistol, sar; me kill him dead, den de Creole gal she no let missee die; if kill me, what um care for dat, ha? if pore missee sabe life. Dat good—dat dam good,—yah, yah, yah!"

And he fell into a convulsion of mirth at the bare idea of sacrificing his own life for his young mistress, an act in which his simple, affectionate heart could find nothing but a capital joke. The men looked gravely—half-ashamed of their own pretentious self-sacrifice—at the glowing black face, and then Jack shouted with boyish enthusiasm—

"Chained to a gun! Poor Mark! who was befriended by the pirates when he fled from the tyranny and oppression of that terrible old martinet, Sir Richard

Varney, when his back was scarred by the lash, and his heart maddened by the oppression that makes wise men mad; who took part with them only in his last extremity, and when he was exasperated against all the world. Oh, Mr. Hawser, let us try to save him or avenge him! He is not a pirate now; and whatever he may suffer at others' hands for his past crimes, we at least owe our lives to him. Do let us try to rescue him."

"Avast," returned the old boatswain, drawing his sleeve across his eyes, "Mark was my friend and messmate, and though he has disgraced himself, I wears no gold scraper, I'm not one of his judges, to sit in court-martial, and condemn him to be swung off at the yard-arm. I'd run my head into a shark's maw to save him; but where's the use o' talkin'?"

"The use," retorted Jack, scornfully, "no, there's no use in talking, but in *acting* there may be. I'll tell you what we'll do. I'll put on the young Spaniard's sash and jacket, we'll get into the boat and shove off at once. Pablo, with a dozen of his best hands, all of them Spaniards except the two villains we have just quieted, is on shore, and cannot leave the island, for we will scuttle the boat. The hands in the schooner are Malays, and other raffs of mongrel breed, almost to a man. We can surely outwit them. We will creep in through a port, and as we have files and other implements, may succeed in getting him away, if not I would rather die than not make the attempt."

"Here's my hand, Mr. Rushton," cried Tom Hawser, gallantly. "We'll board 'em by all that's plucky!"

Jack tossed up his cap.

"Away then," he said. "I will at once change clothes with the fellow we garotted so cleverly."

Off he started.

Pomp and Tom hastened after him.

Pedrillo still lay bound and helpless. Thinking they were come to despatch him, he cast an imploring glance upon them, and tried to raise his bound hands to his brow to make the sign of the cross.

They tore off his green silk jacket bedizened with buttons and pendants of massive gold.

Jack slipped it on.

He then wound Pedrillo's red silk sash, enlivened with strands of rich gold, about his own slender waist, and clapped on his sombrero. Very dashing he looked when thus accoutred.

It was now night, and a haze was sweeping up over the " dim, desolate deep."

The three rushed back to the shore; they set to work at scuttling one of the boats.

They soon knocked a hole in her sheathing boards and filled her with stones and sand.

Then they rigged the other boat, and launched her through the surf.

They scrambled into her.

Pomp and Tom seized the oars, and our hero, who, despite his desperate efforts to rally his resources, still felt weak and faint from the effects of his late violent attack of fever, threw himself into the stern sheets.

"Pull away, jolly hearts!" cried the gallant lad, waving his hat. "We will save our friends or perish in the attempt."

Tom and Pomp cheered.

Then, as if awed by the weakness of their united voices, so different from the full hearty shout of a proper complement of men for such a desperate adventure, fell into grim silence.

The oars throbbed through the lapping billows.

Onwards and onwards they sped through the haze and gloom.

Soon the dim, swaying lights of the anchored vessel glimmered dully through the mist, and the boat was rocking beside the dark hull.

All on board was mirth and gaiety, for the weather, though foggy, had turned oppressively hot, and, by the light of the fighting lanterns, the crew were revelling on deck.

"Hold water!" whispered Jack.

The men rested on their oars, and the boat floated under the tier of bristling guns.

"Dar, sar, dar!" whispered Pomp, "Yo see dat light—he dar, sar!"

"Hist!" murmured Jack.

Soon he scrambled into the chains.

Laying hold of the projecting muzzle of one of the guns, he cautiously peered in.

The gun-deck was deserted by the crew.

It contained but one solitary inmate.

Lashed to the gun nearest to the bulkhead of the captain's cabin aft, Ambrose was descried seated upon the ground, his arms folded and his head bent upon his breast.

Jack crept in through the port.

Ambrose raised himself on his arm, and looked round with a startled air.

Jack made a quick gesture.

He bounded to the side of Ambrose.

The seaman stared at him wildly.

"It is I," whispered Jack; "compose yourself, Mark. Your old messmate too is here. We come to save you."

"You are mad!—you are mad!" gasped Ambrose, fiercely, though he clasped the noble boy to his heart with frantic devotion. "This is too cruel; it wanted but this to give death its last dreg of bitterness."

"Death, dear Mark! 'tis far distant. Coward, let me teach you courage," whispered Jack, with deep emotion. "Compose yourself, I say; we have a boat alongside, old fellow, and should I deserve your love if I would not have one try at saving you? Quick, Tom; now's the time!"

The boatswain, who had scrambled in, was at work in an instant, filing the prisoner's chains.

"O Lord!" he gasped; "there's a light on the companion stair. See to it, Mr. Rushton."

"Ay dios, Pedrillo!" cried a sweet voice, and a lady, with a lamp in her hand, started back. "How you frightened me! I thought you were gone ashore with Don Pablo."

"No, senora," muttered Jack, excitedly.

He seized her wrist.

She recoiled, with flashing eyes.

"Esclava! what is this?" she cried, haughtily.

"Ah, senora, mercy!" murmured Jack, sinking on his knees. "You are too beautiful, too gentle-looking, to wish to destroy us."

CHAPTER XXIV.

A WOMAN'S HEART.

DONNA INEZ gazed in amazement at the kneeling boy, who, with upturned face, hands clasped, and pleading looks, entreated her to keep silence.

Altogether the scene was striking and extraordinary; the dark, shadowy gun-deck; the looming, massy carronades; the glare of the lamp-light falling upon the beautiful face of the Spanish girl, glowing in her deep black eyes, dilated with wonder, flashing her seed-pearl teeth, brilliantly sparkling on the star-like gem that lightly heaved upon her soft bosom.

The wild looks of our brave boy-hero, the rich and romantic dress he had assumed, the stern, anxious faces of the men glaring through the outer gloom.

"Ave Maria!" gasped Donna Inez, pressing her little quivering hand over her throbbing heart. "Who are you, stranger?"

"No enemy, senora," returned Jack, promptly. "I am one of the survivors from the barque 'Titania,' that was boarded and burned by the captain of this vessel; we have come to rescue our countryman, Mark Ambrose, who saved my life. We throw ourselves upon your mercy, senora; do not bring the stain of bloodshed upon your hands; if we are murdered you will be responsible to your own conscience. But, you are a woman; you will not, you cannot, desire the destruction of those who never wronged you."

Donna clasped her hand to her forehead.

"And *he*, Pablo, mi querido!" she murmured, through her quivering lips. "He burned the good ship—killed—killed all her brave crew? He? Ay dios! Oh, Virgin, pity me!"

She sank upon her knees, and hid her face in her hands.

A convulsive shudder thrilled through her delicate form, and then she rose suddenly and thrust back a mass of her heavy black tresses over her snowy shoulders.

"How came you here?" she asked, quickly, her face white with anguish, but her voice proud and firm.

"Through yonder port, senora," returned Jack, in a rapid undertone. "We stole one of the boats we found on the shore; it lies alongside this vessel. Our case is desperate; you see we are armed——"

"Ha! do you dare threaten me?" cried Inez, drawing herself up with the fire and majesty of Medea.

"No, indeed, no, senora," whispered Jack, eagerly and respectfully. "We would rather die than injure you; but we trust to your generosity, to your goodness of heart. Suffer us to escape —retire to your cabin—do not betray us."

"Don Pablo would kill me!" returned Inez, with a shudder.

"Senora," cried Ambrose, rising on his knees, and holding out his hands beseechingly, "hear me one word. You have already stood between me and death. This morning the senor offered to spare me, on condition that I should return to his service. If you will save this mad, rash boy, I will consent to be a slave, a pirate—what you will; but, for his mother's sake, senora—he, her only son; she, a widow—if you would not be branded as a remorseless fiend, if you have one spark of womanly sympathy in your heart, let him go! I will remain, your slave, I say—eager to execute, without question, the senor's darkest commands—save him, senora, it is all I ask!"

"Bueno! if you will swear to keep your promise," returned Inez.

"No, no; never shall you swear such an oath for me!" exclaimed Jack.

He folded his arms, and seated himself doggedly on a carronade slide.

"Si, si, senora—by all that is binding I swear it—only save the lad!" cried Ambrose, eagerly.

"Then my blood be upon your head, Mark Ambrose," returned Jack, "I will not purchase life at such a price!"

"Go, then, lad—the senora will not stay you—heed not me, I know how to face death—Heaven knows that I long for its coming!"

"Paz! silence!" cried Inez, raising her hand.

There was a dead hush.

A step was heard on the companion stair!

Inez flew thither.

"Go!" she cried, quickly. "I cannot see you butchered before my face! Escape! I will save you if I can—but lose not a moment! A Dios!"

With this she darted up the stair, leaving the lamp upon the floor.

Jack and Tom Hawser set earnestly to work, and in a few moments they had freed Mark Ambrose from his fetters.

They crept cautiously to the port.

They peered out.

The negro's white teeth and eyeballs were all that could be distinguished through the darkness.

Ambrose was the last to leave the ship.

He cast one backward glance.

The quick tramping of feet was heard, and a number of half-drunken ruffians came pouring down the hatchway.

"Ola!" roared one of them, savagely. "The prisoner is escaping!—tirad! fire!"

A bright red glare, the thunderous report of musketry, then a wild, piercing shriek!

But, unscarred, the bold Ambrose sprang down into the boat, and, seizing the oars, he and his brave comrades pulled away for dear life.

CHAPTER XXV.

THE FUGITIVES ARE SAVED FROM A WATERY GRAVE.

THROUGH the mist throbbed the little bark, swiftly propelled by the vigorous efforts of the three men and the boy.

All on the deck of the pirate schooner was bustle and confusion.

The air rang with shouts of rage and consternation, as the pirates, terribly alarmed for the consequences of what had happened, rushed to the davits, in order to lower the quarter-boats and give chase.

A blue light was fired on the vessel, haloing her in a violet glare of light, and causing the waves around her to sparkle with electric brightness.

The fugitives were now descried, tugging like mad at the oars.

A yell from the pirates.

Pistols, carbines, linstocks, blazed at them.

Then a gun was pointed.

A cloud of white smoke burst from the dark hull of the schooner, and then followed a tremendous roar.

A heavy shot came spanking past the bows of the boat, and sank in a fountain of spray that glittered like a shower of steel beads.

Maddened to desperation, the fugitives tugged at the oars, and their little craft bounded along through the furrowy billows and was soon buried in the deep darkness that encircled the span of blue light thrown by the illumination on board the schooner.

But though our adventurers were obscured from the view of their terrible foes, they were able to see distinctly all that was going on alongside the schooner.

Men were descried leaping like cats into the boats, and soon a hot chase commenced.

The fugitives maintained the most profound silence, breathlessly struggling against the heavy swell, and finally distanced their pursuers.

After an hour's violent exertion, as if by mutual, tacit consent, they rested their weary arms.

Still the boat drifted on, for, though the wind had not freshened, the sea began to roll heavily under the gunwales.

Suddenly Ambrose uttered a shout.

"Starn all! We have shoaled our water, mates!"

"Eigh! Gorramighty — harkee dat!" groaned Pomp.

It was pitch dark.

The fog was dense and choking, and the seas came swinging against the shuddering sides of the boat.

But the sound to which Pomp had called attention was that dull grating so dreadful to a seaman's ears.

"My limbs, messmates, we're run aground!" cried Tom Hawser, in dismay.

"We are stuck fast on a bank!" shouted Jack.

"O lud, massa!" gasped Pomp,

"THE CARRYING OFF OF LADY MARION VARNEY BY PABLO, THE PIRATE CHIEF."

" what yo call bank, eh? Dis one cuss reef—we all go to lilly piece. Oh, massy !"

But Ambrose rose on the thwart, and, striking the blade of his oar against the top of the coral reef, waited for the next head-wave, which came bouncing astern, with a ruffianly roar, and tossed the frail bark forward.

She cleared the reef, and cracked on bravely.

But Mark's oar was shivered to splinters, and the boat shipped a heavy sea.

The men baled with their hats, but it was soon evident that she had sprung a leak.

For hours they worked desperately.

Their most strenuous efforts barely served to keep them afloat.

A night of peril, toil, and horror wearily passed.

The morning broke at length, the fog cleared, and the sun rose in blazing splendour.

Fortunately, the wind had fallen, and the sea was calm.

Still their condition was dreadful.

They had drifted away, at least a mile from shore, and, spite of their exhaustive labour, the boat was more than half full of water.

" Land right ahead !" shouted Jack, suddenly.

A low coral reef appeared, about a cable's length ahead.

" Hurrah !" shouted Tom. " We are saved, lads !"

The boat was fast settling down.

" Overboard, all of you !" cried Mark ; " we must swim to the reef."

" Sail ho !" shouted Jack.

" Where, where ?" cried Tom.

" Abeam of us, to windward !" rejoined Mark, gloomily. " See, 'tis the frigate."

He fixed a stern glance upon the distant vessel, his cheek grew pale, then his brow flushed.

" It is the ' Fearless !' " cried Jack.

" Aye, lad, and her captain is my bitter foe ; and were he not, I am a pirate and must not look for mercy."

He pondered for a moment, and seemed quite forgetful of the peril of the situation.

Suddenly he lifted his eyes to our hero's face.

" Can you swim, lad ?" he asked, eagerly.

Jack cast a doubtful look at the white, foaming breakers.

" No ; that is—only a little," he said, with hesitation.

Now, Jack was a famous swimmer.

Then why was he guilty of this fib ?

He caught the meaning of Mark's gloomy look, and the drift of his question.

He perceived that it was the intention of Ambrose to plunge into the waters, and drown himself, in order to escape the shameful fate which awaited him in the event of his being taken aboard the English cruiser.

" It must be ! It is my fate," he murmured, vacantly ; " I cannot escape it. Better it should come thus than otherwise."

Then he rose, and stretched out his arms to the boy.

" Come, lad," he said, " grapple me ; I will bear you to the reef."

Jack gave him his hand.

Together they sprang into the water.

Ambrose had wound his left arm about the boy's slight waist, and with the right, struck out lustily.

They had reached the reef in a very few moments, and at no slight peril of being dashed against the sharp edges of the rocks, for the breakers bowled against them in heavy masses.

Pomp and Tom Hawser had already got on to the reef and assisted their companions.

The boat had sunk, and but a few of her timbers, her tiller and oars, floated on to the reef.

Jack seized an oar and turned his eyes eagerly in the direction of the frigate.

There she lay, so near, that it was possible to distinguish the men on the deck.

The morning sunbeams burnished her bellying sails, and glistened on her tapering masts, and on the rich, rippling pennants that twined like flying serpents far aloft amid the roseate clouds, and upon the dear old Union Jack that fluttered at the peak.

Her main-braces were hauled in, and the main-yard thrown aback, and the main-topsail lay to the mast; in fact, she was "hove to."

"Thank God!" cried Jack. "We are seen! We are saved! Hurrah, boys, for Old England!"

Nevertheless, he untied his, or rather Pedrillo's, red silk sash, and, tying it to the blade of the oar, waved it round his head with frantic exultation.

"Hurrah! hurrah!" shouted Tom and Pomp.

Mark Ambrose, however, did not participate in his companions' glee, but stood darkly eyeing the vessel.

Soon a large boat was seen pulling towards them through the glittering water.

The sunshine flashed on the gold band of the mid's cap, who was sitting in the stern-sheet.

Soon the boat came nearer, and at length lay alongside the reef.

"Boat ahoy!" cried Tom, rather unnecessarily, while he rubbed his hands and chuckled.

"Hullo!" responded the midshipman, laughing. "What cheer, hearties! Who are ye?"

"Bless yer eyes, sir, officers and gentlemen," returned the boatswain, cheerily, "belonging to the barque 'Titania,' as was captured by pirates."

"Didn't I tell ye so, Austin?" said the mid, appealing to the coxswain. "These are some of the poor chaps escaped from the wasps' nest yonder."

"Aye, aye, sir," returned the coxswain. "This is a stroke of luck, for now we shall larn the whereabouts of that cussed schooner!"

"Jump in, my men," cried the mid, with a slight swagger. "Yonder vessel is His Majesty's frigate, the 'Fearless,' Captain Sir Richard Varney."

At the mention of this name our hero cast down his eyes, while Ambrose scowled darkly.

They got into the boat.

Tom and Pomp were so delighted at this deliverance from all their dangers and troubles that they could not refrain from shaking hands with as many of the hearty, honest-looking tars as happened to be within reach.

The boat's crew responded very good-naturedly, laughing and cheering the while.

Ambrose was the only one who showed no signs of satisfaction.

He slunk into the boat with the air of a condemned man about to be carried to the place of execution.

"My eye!" shouted the coxswain suddenly, as he caught a glimpse of Mark's dark countenance, "that chap is our old shipmate, Mark Ambrose, as deserted!"

This announcement caused a general exclamation of surprise. Every eye was turned upon the pirate.

Ambrose bent his head on his breast, as if ashamed to look his old companions in the face.

"Surely, my hearty, you must be mad to put your head in the lion's mouth," said the coxswain, gravely; "if we take you aboard, you know what your fate will be."

"Silence, sir!" cried his officer, sternly.

"But harkye, Mr. Middleton," returned the sailor, in a half whisper, "the poor chap desarved pity; let him stay ashore, sir; there's no need as we should bring about—you know what, sir. He can swim to land from the reef, sir; let him bide where he is."

"Impossible," returned the young officer, decisively; "our movements are watched from the ship. Besides, it is his own fault, and we must do our duty. Pull away, lads!"

CHAPTER XXVI.

FACE TO FACE.

UPON reaching the vessel, and getting on board, our adventurers were received with much curiosity by the officers and men.

Ambrose was immediately recognised, and his presence excited no small amount of astonishment.

A whisper passed round, and everybody looked at him pityingly; but all drew respectfully aside as the captain advanced.

He was a short, slight, wiry old fellow, with a sour-looking visage, a keen grey eye, and a shock of silvery hair.

He was primly dressed, and looked what he was, a narrow-minded, cold-hearted, precise personage. He seemed part and parcel of the ship itself, which was a model of neatness and order, the decks being holystoned to a pitch of neatness that was almost painful to the sight, while every rope and spar was adjusted with the greatest nicety.

The adventurers saluted the little magnate with awe and reverence.

With the exception, however, of Mark Ambrose, who folded his arms, and turned aside his head.

"Who is that man?" said the captain, sharply.

"Mark, the captain speaks to you,"

whispered Jack, nervously plucking his companion's sleeve.

Very slowly the seaman raised his black eyes, and fixed them steadfastly upon the captain's face.

There was nothing defiant in the look; the countenance of the wronged but guilty man was perfectly composed, yet a thrill of awe ran through the veins of the bystanders as they watched the direction of that stern, steady glance.

The captain turned scarlet.

"How, sir! Why, yes! You are the mutineer, the deserter, Mark Ambrose."

"Aye, Sir Richard," returned the other, in a deep voice of piercing sternness, "I am Mark Ambrose."

The captain gasped with passion and astonishment at the coolness of his former victim.

He tried to quell him by a stern and fierce look, and certainly there was something very formidable in the glitter of those deep-set grey eyes.

But Ambrose was unmoved; he stood mute and motionless; his manner, though quite calm, was by no means disrespectful.

Finding that he could make no impression upon this ancient rival in love, by his hectoring frown, he gave way, and burst into a rage.

"And do you dare, sir——"

Ambrose interrupted quietly.

"I dare nothing, sir. You say I am a mutineer and deserter; you say no more than is true; with deep shame, as a man and a seaman, I plead guilty to the charge. I am worse than a mutineer and a deserter, I have been guilty of piracy."

"A pirate!" cried officers and men, involuntarily.

"I surrender myself, Sir Richard," rejoined Mark, instinctively touching his forelock. "Let me be punished according to law for my crimes! BUT ——"

Here he sank upon his knee, and clenching his hand, gnashing his teeth, and upraising his eyes to heaven, he went on with passionate vehemence,

"It hath been said by the just Judge, in whose presence I may soon stand, and on whose mercy alone I can rely, for I neither look for nor deserve mercy from man; it hath been said by that just Judge, 'Woe to him by whom the offence cometh.' I charge you before this dread tribunal with driving me—weak and vile as I was to be driven—to become what you call me, a mutineer, a deserter, and, as I add myself, a pirate!"

"The—the villain!" gasped Sir Richard.

Ambrose rose with calm dignity.

"I have spoken," he said; "I yield myself; do what you will with me."

"You shall hang, miscreant!" blustered the furious captain, as he shook his fists; "hang, hang!"

"I would most humbly advise you, Captain Varney," returned the seaman, with a smile of disdain, "if you have any respect for your own dignity, not to sentence your prisoner until he is condemned."

"Good heavens!" groaned the captain as if stunned by the unparalleled calmness of the daring fellow. "Take him away! Send for the quarter-master—

put the pirate thief in irons — take him away !"

"If you please, captain," pleaded Jack, throwing himself before the incensed old man.

"Silence, sir," roared Sir Richard, stamping his foot.

He rushed past; then, after taking a few steps, he paused, as if conscious that he had wholly compromised his dignity, and, intending to return, that he might, by a few cool words, recover his lost ground; but then, as if afraid to trust himself to the influence of his temper, he rushed on, and plunged down the after hatchway.

Poor Jack was aghast at what happened.

"Ambrose," he exclaimed reproachfully, "I can scarcely pity you; you have provoked your fate—you have destroyed yourself !"

"Be easy, lad," returned the other, with an affectionate smile; "you are safe now, and I shall die happy; remember your promise, and so shake hands with me—for the last time—before I don the felon's bracelets."

Jack seized his hands, and grasped them with genuine warmth and gratitude.

"And I have brought you to this, Mark !" he murmured, brokenly.

"Not you, boy, not you," returned the man, shaking his head; " 'tis that eternal justice which is sure to overtake the guilty. I am glad, right glad, that things have fallen out as they have. I have no right to live; it is much better I should die; aye, aye, much better !"

Jack tried to speak, but felt choked with emotion.

"God bless ye, lad, God bless ye; you'll sometimes think kindly of old Mark, who stood your friend when you were *alone in the Pirates' Lair*; you'll sometimes think of him when all is over, won't ye now? Why, then, God bless ye !"

He relinquished the boy's drooping hands, and, while the manacles were being placed round his own wrists, gazed at him with almost womanly tenderness.

Then, falling smartly into his place between the marines, drawn up, with their loaded firelocks on their shoulders, he smiled, and marched off with his guard, as carelessly as if he were unconscious that his hours were numbered.

Conducted by the guard, he paced through the lower deck.

It happened that some alterations were being made in the captain's cabin, and some of its furniture and fittings were lumbered upon the deck; and against the bulkheads, amongst the rest, was a full-length portrait of a young and beautiful girl.

Before this picture he suddenly paused.

The marines seemed instinctively to humour him, for they lingered a moment.

His face grew ashy white, and he looked long and earnestly upon the well-known features.

Then he drew a deep sigh, and, resuming his air of sullen indifference, paced on.

CHAPTER XXVII.

THE FLIGHT OF PEDRILLO.

GREAT was the rage of the fiery Don Pablo, when, arriving, after a long and fruitless search for the fugitives, at the spot where he had left the boats, he found Pedrillo bound, gagged, and utterly powerless, and his two sentinels lifeless, to all appearance.

He was absolutely mad with fury.

He questioned Pedrillo.

The boy, beside himself with terror, made out the best story he could, and gave a terrific account of his desperate struggle with at least a dozen antagonists, declaring that Jack and Tom had enlisted a party of Indians in their service.

Don Pablo did not look upon this story as being altogether improbable, as several flying proas, manned by the aborigines, had been sighted, both by his own party and by Balthazar's, during their exploration of the island.

He found one of his boats scuttled and sunk in the water.

The other had vanished.

The negro and the Malay, bound hand and foot, lay huddled under the rocks, and, when released from their bonds, were found to be in a desperate plight.

The negro's thick skull was fearfully gashed, while the Malay had been half strangled.

They could give but an incoherent account of the attack that had been made upon them, but concurred in Pedrillo's story about the Indians.

It was after sunset that Pablo had returned to the spot whence he started on his search for the fugitives, and the night had set in, hot, close, and foggy.

He was in no small dilemma, having so many men on shore, and no boat in which to transport them to the vessel.

A gun was fired from the schooner.

The pirate chief ordered a fire to be kindled on the summit of a hill, that might serve as a beacon to guide the boats from the vessel which might put ashore in search of him.

But no boats came for a long time, during which the fury of the pirate vented itself upon Pedrillo and the two sentinels, whom he abused, and even struck, in his passion.

At length, just as the morning was breaking, two row-boats, each containing at least twenty-five men, were seen pulling in shore.

They landed, and appeared much worn with fatigue and agitation.

They belonged to the party who had been chasing our adventurers after their escape from the schooner.

Don Pablo at once discerned by their gloomy looks that something was amiss.

He questioned them with respect to the British cruiser.

They exchanged frightened glances.

Neither of them could summon courage to tell the tyrant that Ambrose had slipped the chain.

They said that one of the flying proas, coasting round the island, had brought them intelligence that the frigate had been lying off the other side of the island; but that she had now steered away.

Don Pablo stepped moodily into the boat.

It happened that Fra Valdez, the priest, was one of the party.

Sancho whispered something in his ear, which made the infamous-looking old rascal start, turn pale, and draw his cowl over his face.

The pirate, gasping with excitement, alternately crossing himself, and wringing his hands, gave the monk an account of the escape of Mark Ambrose.

The priest listened tremblingly.

Sancho, in a whine of entreaty, besought him to break the matter as gently as possible to their angry chief.

With much circumlocution, and many softening expressions, Fra Valdez revealed the secret to Don Pablo.

The chief said little.

Folding his arms, grinding his teeth, and shuddering with suppressed passion, he listened.

His silence was even more terrible than his storm of passion.

An occasional deep and bitter curse burst from his white, compressed lips.

Upon getting on board he went straight to the cabin of Inez.

She bounded to meet him, and tried to clasp him in her embrace.

But sternly bidding her be silent, and pointing to a couch, he ordered her to remain in the cabin till he should give her permission to leave it.

Pedrillo had followed him down the companion, and, softly treading in his steps, listened with horror to his stern and savage tones.

Don Pablo stepped out of the cabin.

Pedrillo slipped behind a bulkhead.

The pirate chief slammed to the door of his wife's berth, and locked her in.

Then, with a fierce step, he ran along the gun-deck, and stepped up the companion.

No sooner was he gone than Pedrillo cast one wild look around him, and, slipping through a port, dropped into the main-chains, from which he sprang into the water, and was swimming to the shore.

Striking out with great desperation, he was soon at some distance from the ship.

A yell borne faintly over the smooth sea caused him to turn his head.

Three dark bodies, suspended by the neck, swung writhing aloft at the fore yard-arm.

Pedrillo plunged down through the glassy waters, and, diving along till he was quite out of breath, rose once more to the surface.

He cast one look behind him.

Three bodies swayed stiffly at the yard-arm, and he knew that the savage chief, disappointed of his prey, had wreaked his vengeance upon the African and the Malay, and Fernando the Spaniard, who had the special charge of Mark Ambrose.

Rushing through the surf and scrambling up the shore, the affrighted boy bounded off to the mountains.

After this tragedy the schooner, "every rag set," was run into Canton Bay, and here she anchored.

Leaving his vessel, and disguising himself as a wealthy merchant, Don Pablo fitted out the polacca, and, taking with him a party of picked men, he started for Guam, and, after a day's sail, arrived at San Ignacio, in order to learn what he could of the movements of the British frigate and the intentions of the captain.

He had many agents in the town, from whom he learned that Lady Marion Varney was staying at the governor's house; he resolved to carry her off.

How he accomplished his purpose will be told in the next chapter.

CHAPTER XXVIII.

HOW DON PABLO BORE OFF LADY MARION.

THE Spanish settlement on the island of Guajan consisted of a number of white houses, defended by a couple of forts.

The coasts of the island are rugged, high, and shelving, and the little town lies nestling among the luxuriant foliage of the richly-wooded rocks.

Upon the evening of the third day after his arrival at this place, Don Pablo, and two of his most confidential fellow ruffians, met at a little wine-shop, kept by a burly, black-browed rascal, who had formerly belonged to the pirate gang, and had been set up in business by the liberality of his former commander, in whose pay he still remained as a spy and informer.

It was a glorious evening, and the scene was one of unsurpassed loveliness.

The pirates were seated on an exquisitely rustic balcony that overhung the sea.

Behind rose the lofty mountains, whose romantic peaks were bathed in the soft, rich beams of sunset, here tinged with crimson, there deeply purpling, their hues as bright and changeful as the colours in a prism, their bases finely mantled with forests of palm, mangroves, guavas, bananas, cocoas, oranges, and limes.

Above, the azure heavens were speckless, while below, and stretching far before them, a million billowets flashed like living jewels in the bright beams of the parting sun.

The pirate chief, with Sancho and Fra Valdez, the priest, beguiled the time by smoking their cigaritos, and imbibing freely of Jose's Madeira.

"Canamba!" growled the pirate chief, savagely, as he tossed aside his cigarette, and leaping upon his feet, walked up and down in his usual impetuous manner. "Where is this accursed villain?"

He walked to the door of the wine-shop.

"Jose, Jose!" he shouted, stamping his foot.

The burly wine-seller rushed out in great trepidation.

"Tell me, diabalito," growled the pirate, seizing him by the collar, "did you not say that Gonzalves would be here soon after noon? The convent bells have rung the vespers; where is he, then, you dog?"

"Pardon, senor," cried the frightened host, in a tone of abject servility; "it is not through my fault your lordship has been kept waiting; the fellow assured me that he would be here at the time appointed."

Don Pablo hurled him off with a dreadful scowl, and then walked angrily back to the table.

He twisted his black moustache, gnawed his lip, and beat a tattoo with his fingers upon the table.

Neither of his companions ventured to break the silence.

At length he looked up at the priest, and said, abruptly—

"Padre, why is this? It would seem that the saints have deserted me; all my plans are thwarted—all my enemies escape my vengeance—how is this?"

"Es verdad—that is true, my son," returned the priest, folding his hands across his broad belly, and assuming a grave look. "You have neglected to have masses said for the poor children who fell in the last engagement; you have otherwise offended against the ordinances of our holy church."

Don Pablo crossed himself.

"Perhaps you are right," he said, thoughtfully, "I will see to it."

"It is well said, my son," returned the hypocrite, smiling blandly; "and behold how suddenly a token is vouchsafed of returning favour through your good resolutions."

"Ha! where?" said the pirate, quickly.

"No doubt this is Gonzalves, senor," rejoined Sancho, with animation.

A tall, slim, brown fellow, in a handsome livery—a Moreno, or half-caste—came gliding up the steps that led to the verandah.

He bowed gracefully, and avowed himself his lordship's humblest slave, and eager to learn his lordship's pleasure.

"Carajo!" laughed the pirate, "you come late, Gonzalves; but better late than never."

The lackey explained that he had been delayed by unforeseen circumstances, and hoped that his excellency would not doubt his slave's entire devotion and obedience.

"Por amor de dios—speak quickly, amigo," interrupted the pirate. "Is all well?"

"Si, senor, all is well."

"Ha! and have you carried out my orders?"

"To the letter, senor," returned the man. "The Senora Inglesa can be carried off as easily as a bunch of grapes from this vine."

"Muy ben!" growled Don Pablo, rubbing his hands. "And the potion?"

"Was administered, senor; I took care for that. Don Miguel gives an entertainment to-night and——"

"Maldito! Then his house is full of company?"

"Si, senor; and it was with much difficulty that I could get away from the banquet chamber to attend your excellency."

"Another mischance!" groaned the pirate.

"With pardon, senor, nothing better could have happened for your gracious purpose," returned Gonzalves, smiling. "The Senora Inglesa, overpowered by the potion which I had mixed with her coffee, pleaded headache and drowsiness, and leaving the gay assembly retired to her own apartment, where, I understand from her maid, Juanita, she is sleeping profoundly, having thrown herself upon a couch, quite overcome by the effect of the drug."

The rascal smiled and bowed and bowed and smiled with great humility.

"But, if the place is full of people, how shall we be able to carry out our plans?" asked the pirate.

"Nothing easier, senor," was the answer. "The company have all retired to a distant part of the gardens to witness a display of fireworks; the senora's apartment is situated upon an opposite side of the house; her window, which is reached by a verandah with steps, looks out upon an orange grove."

"Si, si; I know the spot well," rejoined Don Pablo; "and while the caballeros and senoritas are engaged in their revels we will break into the cage and bear off the pretty bird. With such a hostage in our hands we can make what terms we please with those British thunderers. 'Tis a fine plot, amigos."

The pirates murmured their approbation.

"How many men, senor, will you require for this service?" asked Sancho.

"Yourself and the padre, Francisco and Pedro. But stay! is the senora alone?"

"She has but one attendant, and that a female," replied Gonzalves.

"And who is she?"

"Her Spanish maid, Juanita."

"And is she to be trusted?"

"No fear of that, senor," returned the fellow, laying his hand upon his breast, smirking and bowing. "She is my affianced, and entirely loyal to your excellency."

"Bueno!" rejoined the pirate chief, with satisfaction. "If she acts discreetly, she shall be well rewarded; and so, let us be going at once. Sancho, fetch hither your comrades."

The man hurried away.

In a short time he returned, accompanied by a dozen of the gang, who had been carousing indoors.

Don Pablo gave certain orders to his men, and then, taking with him the priest and three other ruffians, he started off on his dark mission.

The sun had now sunk below the horizon, the moon had risen in unclouded splendour, and the heavens glittered with glorious stars.

Don Pablo and his companions, preceded at some distance by the treacherous Gonzalves, passed through the little vineyard at the back of the wine-shop, and entered a narrow, steep lane.

On one side was a high bank, surmounted by palms and bread-fruit trees; on the other, the wall which formed the

"THE COWL FELL DOWN, REVEALING THE STERN FACE OF MARK AMBROSE, WHO FIXED A GRIP ON DON PABLO'S THROAT."

boundary of the grounds of the governor's mansion.

Here Gonzalves stopped, and cast a hurried glance up and down the moonlit vista.

All was quiet; the bright path was chequered with the delicate tracery of the shadows that fell from the multiform foliage quivering aloft in the purple sky, and pierced here and there by the glittering streak of some brilliant planet.

Don Pablo pulled his sombrero down over his brow, and wrapped his mantle round him.

Fra Valdez and the two seamen clustered close together.

Gonzalves took a key from his pocket, and applied it to the lock of an arched door in the masonry.

"Stay here a moment, senor," whispered the traitor. "I will go first, and see that all is safe."

So saying, he passed through the door and re-closed it.

The pirates drew back.

They listened anxiously to his retreating footsteps.

After a few moments of suspense, the door was once more opened, and Gonzalves appeared.

"All is safe," he said, in an undertone. "Follow me, senors, as softly as foot can fall."

Don Pablo and his confederates slipped into the garden, and, taking good care to keep within the shadows of the thick-set trees, crept stealthily after their rascally guide.

The scene was supremely beautiful and peaceful; the white walls and green verandahs of the house glared out in the moonshine, at one end of a little verdant lawn, in the centre of which a warbling fountain jetted its silver spray in the perfume-laden air; while the other sides of this open space were fringed with rows of dark-leaved orange trees burdened with golden fruit, and in the dark recesses of the orange grove a cloud of fire-flies glided and wheeled, rising and falling like floating stars.

Gonzalves now had his hand upon the balusters of the quaintly-carved stairs which led up to the verandah.

He stole up to the folding window, which was partly open, and, moving aside the half-drawn curtains with one hand, peered in.

The room was richly furnished, and upon a couch, beneath a gold-embroidered canopy, the hapless Lady Marion reclined, steeped in profoundest slumber.

"Padre," said the pirate chief, addressing himself to the priest, "you have the phial with you?"

"I have, my son," returned the priest, with a leer, as he produced a little bottle from under his cassock.

"Good," said Don Pablo; "should she awake we may find it useful to silence her."

The priest nodded.

"Sancho?"

"Si, senor."

"Take off your scarf, and hold it in readiness to bind her if she struggles."

The pirate undid his silk sash, and held it loose in his hands.

"Pedro, station yourself in the verandah, under the shade of the lime-tree, and keep a sharp watch upon the gardens."

Gonzalves now descended the steps.

"Is she still asleep?" asked the pirate chief, in a whisper.

"Si, senor; deep as death."

"Up, then," returned the pirate. "Keep close behind me, comrades, and obey my signs. Not a word must be spoken."

Gonzalves turned ashy pale, and walked away on to the lawn, and looked anxiously around.

All was quiet, save that, wafted on the stealing breeze, came the distant strains of music, the murmur of voices, and the occasional rush and pop of a bursting rocket.

Don Pablo entered the chamber.

His confederate villains kept close behind him.

Treading as softly as a creeping panther, he stole upon his unconscious victim, and bent over her.

His dark eyes glistened, and a pinky flush glowed on his olive cheek as he contemplated the beauty of the sleeping lady.

"She is ours," he whispered exultingly. "Be ready, Fra Valdez."

Kneeling down beside the couch he passed his arm round Lady Marion's waist, and softly raised her from the pillow.

She moved, and a convulsive shudder passed through her delicate form, and a sob burst from her parted lips.

In an instant the priest applied the phial to her lip, and she sank heavily in the pirate's embrace.

Don Pablo lifted her from the couch, and supported her drooping form upon his shoulder.

A cloak was instantly thrown around her, and secured by the sash.

Meantime, Sancho was busy securing the jewels and other portable articles of value that were in the room.

When all was ready, Don Pablo stepped nimbly on to the verandah, preceded by Pedro, with his musket on his shoulder, and followed by Sancho and the priest.

They descended to the lawn.

Trembling with fear and suspense Gonzalves awaited them.

Upon seeing that the ruffians had, thus far, at least, accomplished their villanous purpose without let or hindrance, he drew a deep breath of intense satisfaction, and, beckoning them to follow, plunged into the orange grove.

Conducted by the treacherous servant they passed rapidly along beneath the deep shadows of the trees, and emerged through the little door into the lane without the gardens.

"All has gone bravely, senor," said Gonzalves.

"Si; you have acted well in this matter, amigo," answered the pirate chief. "This good service shall not be forgotten."

"Muchissimas gracius, senor," rejoined Gonzalves, smiling; "many thanks."

"Should anything unpleasant result from this affair, you can take shelter with Jose," said Don Pablo, "and so, adios."

"Buenos noches, senor el capitan," returned the fellow, bowing; "good-night, senor captain."

"Have you had a quiet watch?" asked Pablo, of the sentinel without. "Has any one passed?"

"A *boy*, senor," returned the man; "but as he evidently belonged to the house, we suffered him to pass unmolested."

"So much the worse," growled the chief; "but it's no matter now."

Don Pablo and his companion at once proceeded to the wine-shop, which they entered by a back entrance.

Jose received them with obsequious politeness.

"Sancho, call together our comrades," said the pirate chief.

A dozen swarthy villains trooped into the room.

"Is all prepared?" asked Don Pablo.

"Si, senor; the polacca lies moored at the water-steps," replied the men.

"Away, then," said the chief.

Followed by his train, and still bearing the unconscious Lady Marion on his arms, Don Pablo passed out into the little vineyard, and descending a winding pathway down the side of the cliff, came upon a little jetty, abreast of which the polacca was lying.

Don Pablo carried his prize aboard the little vessel, and immediately gave orders that all sail should be set.

In a few moments the light and graceful craft was skimming like a swallow over the sparkling waves of the starlit sea.

CHAPTER XXIX.

PEDRILLO.

THE "Fearless," after cruising for several days among the islands, returned to Guajan, and lay at anchor about a mile from shore.

Extremely indignant, though, perhaps, rather unreasonably, at the treatment his friend, Mark Ambrose, had received at the hands of Captain Varney, and moved by a feeling of compunction at remembering the promise he had made to Donna Inez not to betray the pirate gang, our hero, Jack, had been very reticent as to the whereabouts of the pirates.

More than once a boat's crew had landed upon the pirate's isle, but had failed to discover the lair of the sea-robbers.

On one of these occasions the faithful Snap had been met with on the shore, and the good dog displayed the utmost delight at seeing his young master.

At Jack's request, the animal was taken aboard the "Fearless," and soon became a great pet with the crew.

One morning Jack was summoned to the captain's cabin.

He found Sir Richard seated at a table with a chart and some papers spread out before him.

Mr. Archer, the first lieutenant, a fine, handsome gentleman, stood beside the captain's chair.

Jack saluted the magnate with becoming reverence.

Sir Richard eyed him rather sternly.

"I have sent for you, Mr. Rushton," said he, "in order to ask you a few questions about those buccaneering scoundrels we are in chase of."

Jack bowed.

"To me it appears rather strange that you should have remained so long in the thieves' den, and yet are not able to discover its locality."

"Sir Richard, before replying to your questions," said Jack, "will you permit me to ask your opinion upon a point of conscience?"

The captain stared at the boy.

The first lieutenant smiled.

"Certainly, certainly — speak your mind, boy," said the captain, throwing himself back in his chair, and twitching his lips.

"Then, sir, I must tell you that I gave my word to the wife of the pirate captain that I would not betray the gang."

"In that case, sir, I consider you acted most unworthily," returned Sir Richard, frowning.

Jack's cheek reddened, and his eyes fell.

"The lady—Donna Inez——"

"Ha! Then you saw that romantic person?" said the captain, with an air of curiosity. "I have heard her story from Don Hernandez, the Spanish governor; they say she is a very beautiful woman."

"She is, indeed, a most lovely lady, Sir Richard," replied Jack; "and she appears to be as kind-hearted as she is beautiful. I was in deadly danger, and she aided me to escape; I cannot, for shame, speak a word against one who acted so nobly in my behalf. Her husband is a very fiend; but she is strangely devoted to him. I do not understand how she can love such a miscreant; but I am sure, if she had not been so misguided, she would have been beloved and honoured by every one who knew her. I gave her my word that I would not betray the band; ought I keep my promise?"

"Humph!" grunted the captain; "such a promise ought never to have been made."

Jack turned scarlet; he was about to urge that it had not been given for his own sake, but to save the life of a friend; but he was too generous to allow such an excuse to escape his lips; he remained silent and abashed.

"Then, you mean to say, Mr. Rushton," resumed the captain, after a pause, "that you know where the pirates' lair is situated, and refuse to reveal the secret?"

"Indeed, sir, I know very little about it," returned Jack, bluntly; "I passed but one night in the cavern, and, being allowed the next morning to wander forth into the wood, I ran away."

"And so broke your parole," sneered the captain. "Your nice sense of honour was not touched in that case, eh?"

"I made no promise, sir; I defied the rascal," cried Jack, hotly. "I have no 'nice' sense of honour, sir; I hate the word 'nice' applied in such a sense. I don't pretend to be honourable, I am only blunt and straightforward."

The first lieutenant looked aghast at this display of temper.

"Phew!" whistled the captain. "You are very blunt, sir, very straightforward, and, perhaps, as you say, not very honourable, or you would never have pledged your word to that abandoned woman; but come to the point; you cannot give us any information as to the locality of this nest of thieves?"

"There is one man aboard, sir, who could, and, as I believe, who would conduct you to a secret entrance to the cavern, by which you might reach his treasures, and, perhaps, surprise the gang."

"And who is he?"

"Mark Ambrose, sir."

The captain rose in great anger.

"How dare you, sir," he roared, "mention the name of that ruffian in my presence?"

At this moment there was a knock at the door.

"Come in," said the first lieutenant.

A midshipman entered, and respectfully touched his hat.

"A strange sail along side, sir," he said.

"What is she?"

"A polacca, sir, carrying Spanish colours."

"Have you hailed her?"

"Yes, sir; Don Hernandez is on board of her."

"Ha! say I'll be on deck in a moment."

"Aye, aye, sir," responded the mid.

He saluted respectfully, and left the cabin.

"Retire to the gun-room, Mr. Rushton; remain there till I send for you," said the captain.

Jack bowed, and lost no time in making his escape.

A few minutes afterwards the captain and the first lieutenant went on deck.

Don Hernandez, a noble-looking old man, very handsomely dressed, stepped up to the captain and shook hands with him.

He looked very grave.

"I am deeply grieved to be the bearer of such ill news," he said, in Spanish. "The senora——"

"My wife!" exclaimed Sir Richard, starting, and turning deadly pale. "I know she is weak and ill—but—but——"

He placed his hand before his eyes and staggered backwards.

"It is strange, very strange," gasped the Spanish governor; "the lady has fled, senor, and that in a most mysterious manner. This morning her chamber was found deserted—she is gone!"

"Gone, sir, gone!" shouted the captain of the "Fearless." "S'death, sir, explain yourself."

"I have already told you all I know about the affair, senor," returned Don Hernandez, calmly; "but my servants, Gonzalves and Juanita, were in the secret, as I have since discovered. I have brought them with me; you may question them."

"Where are they?"

"Here, senor."

The two culprits were brought forward.

Gonzalves looked the picture of shame and dismay, Juanita was sobbing bitterly.

She was a very pretty but artful-looking girl.

They threw themselves upon their knees before the stern-faced old man, weeping and wringing their hands.

The captain knit his shaggy grey brows and compressed his lips.

"Speak!" he hissed, through his clenched teeth.

"Ah, senor, pardon—ten thousand pardons," groaned Gonzalves.

"Madre purissima! forgive me, senor," sobbed Juanita. "It was not my fault, indeed."

"No, senor, nor mine, nor mine," rejoined Gonzalves, in choking accents.

"It was not for such as I to oppose her ladyship's pleasure," cried Juanita, burying her face in her handkerchief.

"No, no, the good senor will hold us excused," rejoined Gonzalves, "when all is explained — the senora departed against our wish."

"Zounds, you rascal," raved the captain, aghast, "do you mean to say that my wife eloped—that she left the house of Don Hernandez of her own free will?"

"Si, senor—si, si," whimpered the pair.

"And—was she—was she alone?" gasped the captain, with flaming cheek.

"Si, senor, alone, quite alone," cried Gonzalves.

"You lying dog!" roared Sir Richard, clenching his fists, "you are deceiving me. If I detect you in a lie, I'll have you swung off at the yard-arm, you villain!"

"I, senor, deceive you? No, no, senor, what I tell you is truth—speak out, Juanita, let the gracious senor know all."

"Aye, speak, woman," growled the captain.

"Ay, dios! It is terrible," moaned the cunning girl, clasping her hands. "Last evening, senor, his excellency gave a banquet; at night there were fireworks in the garden. Donna Marianna excused herself from attending the banquet, on the plea of headache and weariness. She retired to her chamber; she did not summon me to attend upon her as usual, so I made bold to follow her, senor; the door was locked, but I—I peeped through the crevice, and I saw her ladyship dress herself in a mantle and hood, and taking her jewels, leave the house by the verandah that faces the orange grove."

"Then her mantle and hood and her valuables were carried off?" said the captain, biting his lips. "So! but how did she get out of the orange grove?"

"Ah, senor—pardon, ten thousand thousand pardons!" moaned Gonzalves, shaking his head and wringing his hands.

"Pardon for what, you scoundrel?"

"I—I gave the senora the key of the boundary gate. She demanded it of me—how could I refuse?"

"It is false, senor!" cried a shrill voice, "false as this lying villain himself who speaks it!"

All started in great surprise.

A slight, graceful youth stepped lightly forward, and bowed with the air of a young prince.

"Who is this lad, Carlos?" asked Don Hernandez, turning to a venerable-looking old man, his steward, standing beside him.

"I do not know, your excellency," returned the old gentleman. "As we were embarking, the boy accosted me, and begged so hard that I would bring him aboard the English frigate, that at length I consented."

The lad was standing in a graceful attitude, his hand leaning lightly upon a short poignard thrust through his belt, and his fine dark eyes fixed sternly upon Gonzalves.

That treacherous scamp glared with blanched face at the boy, and presented a pitiful spectacle of craven fear and conscious guiltiness.

"My name, senor, is Pedrilio," said the lad, with another graceful salute, "and I belong to the crew of Don Pablo, the pirate."

The astonishment caused by this cool announcement may easily be imagined.

The boy remained quite calm and self-possessed, with his eyes bent downwards.

At length, when silence was obtained, he proceeded, with the same nonchalance with which he had commenced,

"I say, senors, that I belong to the crew of Don Pablo's vessel; but I should rather speak of my connection with the pirates as a thing of the past, for, having offended the senor by my negligence when on sentry in the island, and my life being in danger, I leaped overboard and swam to the island. Here I met with a party of Indians, whom I persuaded to carry me over to Guajan, in their flying proa. I lurked among the shipping in the harbour, in hopes of obtaining a berth in one of the vessels, and, one evening, saw Don Pablo, with a dozen or so of his picked men, land at the pier-head. I dogged their steps to a certain wine-shop kept by one of the senor's paid spies. I hid myself in a vine-arbour, and overheard the pirates plot with this fellow, Gonzalves, who is also one of the senor's accomplices——"

"Mercy, senors! do not believe one word this wretch is saying—it is false, utterly false. I can disprove these charges."

Pedrillo kept silence, and allowed the rascal to speak.

"Silence, you scoundrel!" shouted Sir Richard, fiercely. "Proceed, boy."

"It was stated by Gonzalves that he had drugged the lady's coffee, and that, overpowered by the effects of the potion, she had retired early to her chamber, and was sunk in a deep slumber; and it was agreed that he, Gonzalves, should conduct the pirates to her apartment. He guided them to a door in the garden-wall, by which he admitted them to the orange-grove, and thence to the lady's room. I followed the party and was a witness to all their proceedings. Men were posted in the avenue without the garden. I think they saw me, but, mistaking me for one belonging to the household, suffered me to pass without question. I concealed myself behind some trees, and saw Don Pablo and the rest bear away the lady, who seemed to be quite insensible. They carried her aboard the polacca. That is all I know of the affair."

"But why did you not raise an alarm?" asked Don Hernandez.

"There was no time, your excellency. Besides, I dared not move from my place of ambush, or the pirates would have killed me on the spot."

"But have you no witness to prove your identity? to give evidence that you did, indeed, belong to the pirate gang?"

"There is aboard, a young English midshipman, who escaped from Don Pablo's fastness; he will recognise me, I have no doubt."

"Fetch Mr. Rushton," said the captain.

Our hero was called, and came on deck.

He was in no little degree astonished at seeing Pedrillo.

"Do you know this youth, Mr. Rushton?" asked the captain.

"Yes, sir," returned Jack. "He is one of the pirate gang—indeed, it was he whom I and my companion bound and gagged in order to effect our escape. I remember him well."

"What have you to say in answer to all this, Gonzalves?" asked the Spanish governor, sternly.

The traitor called upon all the saints to bear witness to his innocence, swearing that he knew nothing of Don Pablo or his gang, and that the lady had left the house in the manner he had previously related.

His protestations, however, availed him little; he was handed over to the custody of Don Hernandez, who directed that he should be immediately conveyed on shore, with Juanita, and be confined in prison.

Upon hearing this sentence, the Spanish girl shrieked and fainted, and was borne over the side by the Spanish seamen.

As for Gonzalves, he was bound hand and foot, and thrown into the polacca.

The captain, the first lieutenant, Don Hernandez, and our hero then adjourned to the state cabin, where a council of war was held.

The result of the consultation, and the effect it had upon the destiny of Mark Ambrose, with the exciting expedition undertaken by our three adventurers and the faithful Snap, for the rescue of Lady Marion Varney, will form the subject of our next chapter.

CHAPTER XXX.

MARK AMBROSE TO THE RESCUE.

BENEATH the feathery crest of a palm-crowned rock that spurred out from the cliffs of the pirates' island in a sort of horn, or curve, forming a natural barrier against the force of the heavy tidal waves, and rendering the enclosed waters as smooth and calm as a mill-pool, a long-boat, manned by a large party of fine, determined-looking British tars, glided stealthily along, and, penetrating into the innermost recesses of the little creek, ran under a vista of thickly-clustered trees.

The men stepped out of the boat, and gathered around their officers.

The party consisted of Mr. Archer, the first lieutenant, Mr. Middleton, the midshipman, Jack Rushton, Tom Hawser, Pomp, Mark Ambrose, Pedrillo, and twenty picked men of the crew of the "Fearless," and last—and refreshing to state, *least*—the faithful Snap.

Our readers will, perhaps, be somewhat surprised to find Mark Ambrose of the party, but his presence is thus accounted for.

At the council held in the state cabin of the king's ship, respecting the measures to be taken for the recovery of the abducted Lady Marion, our hero had so positively asserted that no one but Mark Ambrose would be able to find the secret entrance to the cave, by which the pirates might be surprised, and had pleaded so hard to the captain that the prisoner should be liberated in order to join the expedition, that consent was at length given, and Mark came on shore with the rest.

The ex-pirate's stern, dark face looked more gloomy and saturnine than ever; his eyes moved restlessly, his lips were tight compressed, and his whole demeanour betokened his anxiety and suspense.

"Silence!" said Mr. Archer, sharply, for the men were conversing in low, excited whispers.

They immediately ceased speaking, and awaited their orders in perfect stillness.

"And you think, Ambrose, that we have effected our landing unobserved by the sentinels along the coast?"

"Aye, sir," returned Mark, in his deep, calm tone.

"And you feel convinced that Lady Varney has been carried off to the cavern?"

"I do, sir."

"But is it not possible that the miscreants have taken her on board the schooner?"

"That's scarcely probable, sir; Don Pablo would not take her into the presence of his wife, who is a very tigress in her jealousy."

"There is something in that," rejoined the lieutenant, with a half smile. "And how, then, are we to proceed?"

"I will go alone," returned Mark, decisively.

"What! alone into the thieves' den?" said the lieutenant, in surprise. "Ha!" he added, his brow contracting, "you may have your own reasons for such a course."

He glanced at the ex-pirate suspiciously.

The ghost of a smile passed over the seaman's stern, swarthy face, and he replied, calmly—

"Unless you can trust me in this matter, sir, my assistance will be of little use to you. There is but one way in which we can get admission into the cave without raising an alarm, and thereby losing our labour, for these rocks are pierced and tunnelled like a rabbit-warren."

"But, hang it, man, surely our party is strong enough to take the place by storm? According to Mr. Rushton's account, the principal entrance to the lair is a large cave on the coast. Let us make a bold attack upon the scoundrels, What say ye, lads?"

"Aye, sir, aye," responded the men, eagerly, and they instinctively fingered their cutlass hilts.

"Avast!" said Ambrose, with a scowl. "Lady Marion would be murdered on the spot by the Malay savages; besides, there is a vault beneath the cavern filled with powder-casks, Greek fire-pots, and other combustibles. A huge stone is poised by sheet chains above the arched entrance, and as soon as you were all entered, the barriers would be lowered, and you would all be caught like rats in a trap."

"The devil!"

"Don Pablo is a desperate and a brave villain," rejoined Ambrose, "and as wily and watchful as a fox."

"Then speak out, man; we are losing time. What is your project?"

"I will go alone to the cave; Pedrillo shall follow with six of the boat's crew."

"But I, Mark, I will go with you," said our hero, firmly.

"No, boy; you have cost me enough trouble already. You shall run no further into danger. I will conduct six of the ablest hands to a spot near the entrance of the cave; I will post them in ambush, and will then go forward and explore the passages that lead to the principal chambers beneath the rocks, find out in which of them Lady Marion is imprisoned, then return to the party, and make further arrangements according to circumstances."

"But you may be discovered and taken," objected the lieutenant.

"I must risk that," said Ambrose.

"And what am I to do with the rest of the men?" asked the officer.

"Let some remain with the boat, the rest take up their position under the cliff, a line of pickets being formed in our wake, so that in case it comes to a brush, our whole force may, by passing the word, be collected upon the point of assault. But nothing must be done rashly. We tread over mines that may burst and blast us at any moment; we are walking, it may be, over our own graves."

This pleasing announcement was delivered in the coolest tone, and did not fail to make some impression upon the sturdy tars, who, brave as they were eager as dogs in the slips for a hot chase, or a battle royal, yet could not help feeling a qualm of fright at their perilous position.

They exchanged uneasy glances, and seemed anxious to move from the spot.

"Listen," said Mark.

With the stock of his musket he struck a slab of rock embedded in the tangled ground weeds. Boom!

"The ground beneath our feet is hollow," said the lieutenant, with a slight start. "The island is volcanic, and a very honeycomb of caves and crannies. Could we not force an entrance here?"

"Aye," returned Ambrose, "and easily, too. 'Tis but to raise that stone."

"Then why not make the attempt?"

"Because there is a loaded carronade beneath it fired by a spring-lock attached to the slab with a chain," he answered. "But come; let us separate, sir. Tom Hawser will go with me."

THE DESTRUCTION OF THE PIRATE SHIP.

"Aye, aye, my hearty," returned the boatswain, gripping his hand. "Lead on, I foller thee, as the play-hactor said to the ghost. Blow me hard, yer honour, I hopes you'll speak a good word for this brave chap, and do your best to get him a free pardon if he succeeds in rescuing madam from these Spanish sharks. Well, sir, I know as 'tarn't my dooty to mention it, and I axes pardon."

With this he touched his forehead, and slunk behind some of his comrades, as if a little scared at his own boldness.

"I am sorry for you, Mark Ambrose," said the lieutenant, with feeling. "You are undoubtedly a brave fellow. What excuse have you to give for disgracing yourself as you have done by joining a gang of such accursed buccaneering wretches? You must have been mad."

"I *was* mad—why? Lashed like a hound—bound like a wild beast—stung to the heart!" growled Ambrose, fiercely. "But, there, I plead no excuse, I ask no indulgence; I will save this lady, if possible, and then—why, let them hang me! I care not; death is welcome. Avast! you will think me such a fool, and see—see how I tremble!"

He stood straining his arms, every muscle quivering, and his face deathly sallow, from the sickening emotions that surged in his tameless heart.

He walked moodily off, apart from the rest.

The lieutenant followed him quickly, and laid his hand on his shoulder.

"You tremble! Is it possible? Does your heart fail you?" whispered the officer.

"Aye, sir," returned Ambrose, in a hoarse murmur; "because *I shall see her face—she will speak to me!*"

Then, stamping his foot to quell his emotion, he resumed his calm, stolid manner, and requested the officer to pick out the six men who were to accompany him.

This was done, Pomp volunteering to join the party.

Jack was most eager to be one of the number, but Ambrose insisted upon his remaining behind.

Directing his companions to keep a respectful distance in the rear, Ambrose sprang up the rocks, and made off in the direction of a thick wood in a valley on the inland side of a tall, romantic peak.

He had not proceeded many steps, when a light, quick patter among the sere giant grass caused him to turn his head. It was Snap.

The dog was bounding after him, sniffing the ground as he went.

Ambrose turned, threatened the dog with his gun-stock, and tried to drive him off.

The next instant Jack Rushton came springing through the bushes, and ran up to Mark's side.

"What now?" growled the ex-pirate, darkly.

"You shall not go without me," said our hero, in a hushed but eager voice; "I know something of the intricacies of the rocky passage. I shall be of use, believe me, Mark."

"Back, get back," returned the other, impatiently waving his hand.

Jack smiled, shook his head in deprecation, and continued to follow.

Ambrose halted suddenly.

Leaning upon his carbine, he looked the boy steadfastly in the face.

"Hark ye, lad," he said, in his deep, stern voice, "I am a man of my word—you'll give me credit for that?"

"Well, well."

"Unless you return at once to Mr. Archer, I swear I will give up this enterprise—I will not stir forward a step!"

"But, Ambrose—"

"You would not alter my resolution if you were to preach for a month!" returned the other, snappishly. "Presumptuous fool! you shall not madly fling away a life that I have striven so hard to save."

"Hist Mark! look yonder," cried Jack, suddenly, in a low, excited whisper.

He clutched his companion by the arm, and dragged him back behind a tree.

The form of a tall man, dressed in a long serge robe, and with a monk's cowl pulled close down over his face, appeared descending the rocky pathway.

"It is Fra Valdez," muttered Ambrose. "Run, lad; let the others approach cautiously. We must secure him."

Jack glided away like a shadow.

CHAPTER XXXI.

THE WOLF IN SHEEP'S CLOTHING.

AMBROSE crept close down upon the flowering sward, under the black shadow of a wide-spreading tree.

The priest came striding along, his eyes bent on the ground, evidently apprehending no danger.

A slight rustle in the bushes, and Ambrose heard the deep breathing of his comrades crouching in the grass close behind him.

Fra Valdez seemed startled too.

He threw back his cowl, and glanced nervously around him.

Ambrose bounded from his covert, and seized the priest by the throat before he had time to comprehend his position, hurled him backwards against a bank, and half strangled him.

"Paz! One whisper, and I will drive this knife through your heart!" growled Ambrose.

"Todos santos! who are you? What does this mean?" spluttered the priest, wrestling fiercely, for he was a powerful man.

He soon, however, gave up the contest when he found himself surrounded on all sides by the stern-visaged seamen, who pointed their pistols to his head and their cutlasses to his breast.

The poor priest was terribly frightened, and, clasping his hands together, invoked all the saints to his aid.

Ambrose repeated his threats, and roughly silenced him.

"What shall we do with the fellow?" asked Mr. Middleton, the midshipman in command of the ambuscade party.

"Hold him fast! brain him if he dares to speak," returned Ambrose, in a tone of terrible ferocity, which made our hero look grave, for it reminded him unpleasantly of Mark's past career.

The seamen, however, who, naturally enough, are always pitiless when dealing with those wolves of the sea, those ruthless scourges, the pirates, kept a savage grip upon the padre's arms.

Ambrose tore open the prisoner's cassock, and, with his knife, cut away a little leathern satchel that depended from the monk's girdle.

"Ha! traitor!" hissed the priest, struggling with the men, and trying hard to reach Ambrose, whom he anathematized with boundless fury and consternation.

But his captors held him fast, and stared with curiosity at Ambrose, who, quite unmoved by the priest's abuse, coolly opened the pouch and drew forth a good-sized key.

A stern smile lit up his countenance.

"This is worth more than all the great guns and small arms aboard the frigate," he said, with a chuckle of satisfaction; "but what is this?" he added, drawing a slip of paper from the pouch.

The priest became frantic, but receiving several admonitory raps on his bald pate from pike handles and pistol-butts, he relapsed into silence, though his breast panted and his legs quivered like reeds.

Written upon the paper, in a fine, delicate hand, were the following words, which Mark Ambrose read and translated:—

"I have determined, Padre, to adopt your suggestion. The Senora Inglesa shall be committed to your charge, and sent away in the polacca, to the place of security you mention. I will write to Don Hernandez, the governor of Guajon, and threaten him that in case of his refusal to liberate my followers, Gonzalves and the girl Juanita, my lady, the prisoner, shall surely be put to death. Come to my private chamber an hour before midnight. The pass-word is 'se pronto' (be ready.)

"PABLO PAREDES."

"Was ever heard tell of such an unconscionable, insolent scoundrel?" cried Mr. Middleton.

"Good!" said Ambrose, thoughtfully stroking his chin. "Hold the precious priest fast," he said, sternly, "and do not suffer him to breathe a word."

He threw off his jacket, and handing his musket to one of the bystanders, tightened his belt, thrusting into it a broad-bladed knife and a pair of pistols.

"Now let me have that wolf's sheep's clothing," he said.

"You may well so call it," returned Middleton. "Tear off his cassock; under the garb of peace and sanctity he conceals the heart of a fiend."

"Aye," returned Ambrose; "he is the worst rogue in the gang. It was he who instigated the Malays to murder the good and pious superior of the monastery at Luzon. I will give Don Pablo credit for thus much, he knew nothing of that affair; there is not a Spaniard of the crew who would have harmed one silvery hair of that holy man's reverend head, excepting this villain, who was expelled from the brotherhood for theft and profligacy."

The honest British tars growled their wrath and abhorrence.

Fra Valdez tottered and sank upon his knees in a palsy of fear, and perhaps of remorse.

His robe was torn off and tossed to Ambrose.

He wrapped it closely about him, tied the cord tight round his waist, and drew the cowl over his eyes.

"Now," said he addressing his comrades, "follow me, stealthily, and at a distance."

The midshipman nodded, and leaving two men to take care of the priest, whom, now silent and passive, they at once dragged off to the boats, they crept after Ambrose, who, imitating the gait and manner of the man whose garb he had assumed, walked slowly and calmly onwards to the little woody valley before mentioned.

At length he paused before a rock in the hill side.

He pushed hard, and after a moment or two the slab gave way, sank inwards, and rolling round upon an iron pivot, displayed a deep, dark shaft.

"Why can't we all rush in and smoke the hornets out of their nests?" whispered the bold midshipman, drawing his pistols.

"Avast!" snarled Ambrose, laying aside, in the fervour of his excitement, his tone of habitual respect when addressing an officer; "stay here; leave the stone half open, it fastens with a spring inside, and may be barricaded; if I am discovered, thrust in the point of a marlinspike; and should you hear my whistle, or the report of a pistol-shot, rush in and show your manfulness, but keep all safe in the rear, so that you can beat a retreat if necessary. Neglect this caution, and you are all dead men."

With this he pushed back the stone and crept into the cave.

No sooner had he entered than Jack made a quick gesture to the officer and the rest, and unobserved by Ambrose, who was groping his way down the rude stone steps, leaving the slab unclosed for an instant in order to profit by the jewelled gleam of bluish moonlight that streamed in.

"That young dog, Rushton, has gone after him!" whispered Middleton. "Call him back!"

"Hold, sir!" returned a wary old seaman. "Don't speak, for heaven's sake! a word may destroy Ambrose. Silence, pray, sir—call him to account arterwards!"

"I will, you may be certain," returned the mid, tossing his head airily; "I won't stand breach of orders from any one under my command. And yet, by George, it *is* a temptation!—this is a delicious adventure!"

CHAPTER XXXII.

THROUGH DANGER AND DARKNESS.

MEANWHILE, Jack was crouching in the dark in a sort of cell or crevice on one side of the rocky tunnel.

Ambrose walked to the end of the passage, and laid his hand against the hard, cold bands and bosses of a heavy door. He crept back again.

Stealing once more up the steps, he pulled the stone that screened the entrance back into its place, excepting that he allowed just a crevice to remain unclosed, through which the steel head of a pike had been thrust from without.

As he re-passed down the steps, his robe brushed against our lurking Jack.

"Ha!" he gasped, starting as if he had trod upon a scorpion, "some one is there—something touched me!"

Drawing his knife he prodded at the wall. Jack narrowly escaped the fate of Polonius behind the arras, for the blade passed between his arm and his side, and clinked against the stones.

He clenched his teeth, and moved not a muscle.

"I must have been mistaken," Ambrose thought, as he groped about in the dark. "I must get a light; the lantern is no doubt in its old place, and I must attend to that spring."

Jack ensconced himself close in the dark crevice.

Feeling along the wall till he came to a niche, Ambrose took therefrom a large horn lantern, which he lighted from a tinder-box that lay beside it.

The dim, yellow light streamed through the rocky vault.

Again he reconnoitered.

"Strange," he muttered, seeing no one near, for Jack was completely concealed in his nook; "I could have sworn that some one touched me. Perhaps it may be a token—they say this place is haunted; spirit hands may be stretched out to warn me. Pshaw! this is no time to indulge in such mad fancies; if I can save *her*, what matters for the rest?"

He then felt along the wall till his hand came in contact with a chain.

"I had forgotten this," he mused; "it is connected with the spring, which will clash to at a touch. Ha! good! it passes through this ring; I will block it with my knife."

Jack watched his movements with breathless curiosity.

He passed the blade of his dagger through a link of the chain nearest to the iron ring, wedging it in such a manner as to render it useless as a means of communication with the spring.

Then, pulling the cowl close down over his face, he walked boldly to the door and knocked.

"Who is there?" asked a voice within, accompanied by the rattle of a musket.

"I, Fra Valdez," returned Ambrose,

imitating the voice of the man he personated.

"Give the word."

"Sé pronto."

"Good; I will let you in directly."

Then was heard the unhooking of chains, the clash of bars, and the shooting of locks.

"Good night to you, padre," said the Spanish sentinel, shouldering his musket. "The senor expects you."

"Benedicte, my son," mumbled the pretended priest. "Conduct me to him at once."

"A word—have you heard the news?" whispered the sentinel, plucking the priest by the robe.

"What news?"

"Carramba! saving your reverence," growled the pirate. "These women will bring us all to destruction. Do you know what has been resolved upon with respect to the English lady?"

"Partly."

"Listen, then."

He led Ambrose a little way down the passage, and gesticulating with great animation, poured an indignant recital into his ears.

Ambrose listened gravely, shading the lower part of his face with the loose sleeve of his cassock.

The door, meanwhile, had been left open.

Jack's quick eyes instantly detected several niches along the walls.

Stepping quickly through the door, he popped into one of these alcoves, unperceived either by Ambrose or the sentinel.

After a few moments' conversation with the pirate, Ambrose walked on.

The Spaniard returned to the door; he did not notice Jack as he passed the dark niche, but set to work at securing the door, a task which took some time.

While he was thus engaged, our hero slipped from out his hiding-place and darted noiselessly—he had taken off his shoes—in pursuit of Ambrose.

He found him standing beside an arched door of a chamber, from within which the sounds of voices could be plainly distinguished.

Jack drew back, and, lurking behind a sort of buttress of rock and rude masonry, listened breathlessly.

"Senora, it must be done," said a stern voice from within the chamber. "You must at once sign that paper."

Mark and Jack both recognised the clear voice of Don Pablo; he was speaking in English, with the slightest foreign accent.

"Never!" returned the lady, decisively, though her voice trembled.

"But if I insist," returned the pirate, with an undertone of ferocity; "you see in what circumstances I am placed; you know something of my character; you are aware of my power. I do not wish to threaten you, senora; but I insist upon your signing this paper, which I shall dispatch to your husband; it is my ultimatum. It contains the terms on which alone you can be set at liberty, or even be spared from death; there can be no doubt that they well be at once acceded to; refuse to sign it, and let the consequence of your perversity rest upon your own head."

"And—if—I refuse to put my hand to this paper—you will—kill me?" gasped the lady.

"I am a pirate, senora," returned Don Pablo, "outcast by the society whose laws I laugh at and defy! Every man's hand is against me, and my hand against every man. It is only by inflexible determination that I can hope to brave the hate, persecution, justice, vengeance, call it what you will, of the whole world in arms against me. I have gathered my sympathies within a narrow circle; I have a wife whom I love, devoted followers whom I must protect; all without that narrow pale are my merciless foes, for whom I have no mercy."

"But surely, wretch as you are—you have a gallant bearing, you have that evil courage which sometimes gives a tinge of dark heroism, even to the criminal—surely you would not wreak your spite upon a weak and defenceless woman?"

"Do not deceive yourself, senora," sneered the pirate; "you are a fair woman—nay, an angel of grace and beauty — as Don Pablo Parades de Alcala I should have been your devoted slave; but, as Pablo the Pirate, I look upon you merely as a hostage; you do not belong to me; you are a pledge of safety to my whole band, and that is a band of Spanish, Chinese, and Malay—pirates. I leave you to suppose what mercy you are likely to expect from such men, when you endanger their lives by a foolish resistance of my reasonable request. Senora, sign the paper."

Lady Marion uttered a wail of despair, and her head sank upon the table.

"You still refuse! I admire your constancy of purpose; it is a quality that I can well appreciate, for it is one for which I am myself distinguished; but I remind you again that I am a pirate, and that I dare not save you; but, senora, I will not appeal to your fears but to your mercy."

"Mercy! for you and yours! Well, perhaps, wretches as you are, if it rested in my power, I would strive to save you, though from punishment so terribly deserved."

"Do you think, senora, that I would plead for mercy for myself or my band?" chuckled the pirate. "Not I!—not we! We neither ask nor give quarter. I ask mercy for one of your own sex—a child, a picture of cherub beauty and innocence."

"A child?"

"Si, senora; perhaps, while you were staying at Garajon you may have heard that the last prize I captured was a merchant barque, the 'Titania?'"

"Yes," returned Lady Marion, in a quivering tone, "I have heard the cruel story. I was well acquainted with poor Captain Transom, whom you ruthlessly murdered, with all of his crew."

"He had his only child on board at the time the ship was taken."

"Nellie! Darling little Nellie Transom!" cried Lady Varney, with a slight shriek. "You would never be such a monster as to harm that innocent little child! I will not believe it! You have, perhaps, a child of your own."

"No; gracios a Dios — No, thank God!" returned the pirate, rather huskily. "But trust me, senora, age or sex, comeliness or beauty, vice or virtue, are conditions which, in the case of my prisoners and hostages, affect me not in any degree. But you can save the child——"

"By signing this letter?" cried Lady Marion, eagerly. "I will! I will! but only on one condition."

"Name it, senora."

"Yes; I will write to my husband, explain my position, beseech him to suffer you to escape, to send you whatever ransom you demand, if you will swear that you will send the poor child with the letter to Guajon."

"I will swear, senora."

"There, there, then!" cried the lady, as she snatched up the pen, and writing hurriedly. "It is done; there is my signature. Respect your oath, for I have named the condition upon which I have sent the message, and if you break faith with me your power over my life shall avail you nothing. No, rather than my husband should spare you, I will die by my own hand!"

"Have no fear, senora," laughed the pirate.

Then he turned towards the door.

"A footstep! Fra Valdez. Come in."

The door opened.

The cowled monk glided into the room.

"You must accompany the good padre," said Don Pablo, with a sinister smile; "he will conduct you to a place where you will be held in safe keeping till the terms of this treaty are confirmed by the senor, your husband."

"But—but where will he take me?" murmured Lady Varney, pale and frightened. Oh, is there no treachery intended?"

She looked at the priest.

He stood still as a statue, the cowl drawn close over his face.

He seemed so weird, so like a familiar of the fiendish inquisition, that she recoiled with dread, and sank upon her knees.

"Oh! sir," she exclaimed, brokenly, "you are a priest, you wear the garb of religion; you will protect me from the dark designs of this terrible man."

The priest stood quivering like a reed in the storm-wind.

Suddenly he sprang forward, he wound his left arm around her waist, and clutched her hungrily to his lone and blighted heart. His cowl fell back; she knew him at once, and uttering a shriek, sank, shuddering in his embrace.

"Ambrose!" yelled Don Pablo. "Ha! traitor, you have destroyed yourself."

The seaman regarded him with that calm, quelling glance, peculiarly his own.

For an instant the pirate chief was taken aback.

The next, recovering himself, he snatched his pistols from his belt.

Putting Lady Varney gently aside, Ambrose bounded upon the pirate, and caught him by the throat with a grip of steel.

The two men wrestled madly.

Lady Varney looked on in horror and bewilderment.

Suddenly, she felt herself seized by the hand. It was our brave hero, Jack, who stood beside her; despite her resistance, he forced her from the chamber, leaving Ambrose and Pablo closed in what seemed a death struggle.

CHAPTER XXXIII.

THE SIEGE OF THE PIRATES' LAIR.

THE struggle between Don Pablo and Mark Ambrose was fierce and protracted.

The two men were not unequally matched; for though Mark was heavier, and perhaps more powerful, than his antagonist, Pablo had the advantage of being younger and more active.

They wrestled with amazing fury for the possession of a dagger which the pirate had drawn.

With that repugnance which an Englishman ever feels at using the knife, even in an encounter of this sort, Mark forebore to seize the advantage, which presented itself more than once, of driving the poignard to the hilt in his foeman's breast.

During the fearful struggle, Mark had prevented Pablo from shouting for assistance, by maintaining that iron grip upon his throat.

At length, enraged and alarmed at the shrieks of Lady Marion and the cries of Jack, who appeared to be contending with the sentinel outside, Mark summoned all his strength, and, closing with Pablo, seized with both hands by the neck, and tightened his grip till the face of the latter became horribly distorted, and he sank upon the earth, limp and senseless.

Then Mark seized a carbine that hung on the wall, and darted through the door.

He found Jack engaged in a conflict similar to that through which he had himself just passed, but one far more unequal; for the brave boy was doing battle with the sentry, whose gun having mis-fired, was attacking Jack with his sword.

It was quite a melo-dramatic combat; for the cutlasses flashed and chinked in a terrific style.

Mark rushed upon the pirate, and beat him down with his musket.

"Take the lantern," panted Mark, as he wound his arm round Lady Marion's waist. "On to the door!—Hark! our shipmates are at work!"

At work, indeed, like a band of Cyclops at Vulcan's anvil.

Their axes and pikes bashed and splintered upon the door, till the echoes roared amain.

"Hurrah!" shouted the blue-jackets.

"Steady, there, men!" shrieked the shrill pipe of Mr. Middleton, the mid. "Fire a shot through the lock; prise open the door with that bar. Steady, men!"

Another element was added to the dismal din.

Clang—bang—boom—chang! rang the tocsin of a gong, accompanied by the most unearthly yells from the pirates, rushing from all parts of the rocky fastness into the main passage.

Mark looked behind him.

A swarm of faces, white, brown and

black, appeared at the end of the dark vista, and came sweeping towards him.

"Down," whispered Mark.

He sprang into one of the dark niches in the wall and crouched low.

Jack instantly followed his example.

Then came a blinding flash and report like the explosion of a powder-mill.

A dozen muskets had been fired, and the bullets "ping" past, and thud into the yielding door.

Once more was heard a crash.

Lady Marion shrieked, and fainted.

"Huzza! Down with the pirate villains!"

With a stirring cheer the British tars came scampering in, like terriers bounding into a rat's run.

The advancing tide of faces suddenly ebbed, and the pirates turned their backs and ran away.

"Forward, men!" shrieked Mr. Middleton. "After the wolves!—down with 'em, lads!"

And, brandishing his cutlass, he bravely led the van.

"Hold!" thundered Mark, throwing himself before them, and seizing Mr. Middleton in his strong arms, much to the disturbance of that young gentleman's dignity. "Not a step! Back, all of you,—run for your lives!"

The caution was well timed; for, with the crash of a falling avalanche, a huge piece of rock bashed down, completely blocking the passage before them, and filling the place with a choking smother of dust and flinty particles.

This was enough.

The bold tars, remembering Mark's former warning, and, dreading to be smothered like bees in a hive, sped away, helter-skelter, tumbling over each other, and madly contending who should be foremost.

They escaped from the cave.

To his honour, be it recorded, the brave little middy, Mr. Middleton, was the last to leave the cavern.

"Keep together, there," he piped. "Hold on! you confounded cowards, will ye?"

The men, as if ashamed of their late panic, gathered in a group.

"Away!" cried Mark, who still bore Lady Marion in his arms. "To the boats!—but not through the wood; keep in the open; give the hills and the bush as wide a berth as you can. Forward!"

"Look out!" cried Jack, suddenly.

A report was heard among the bushes overhead.

A bullet whizzed past Mr. Middleton's cheek.

"Hang their impudence!" cried the little mid, wrathfully, "fire into the bush; give 'em a raker, men."

This order was instantly obeyed.

A volley was poured into the wood-side.

It was followed by a yell.

A Malay bounded like a stricken deer over a thicket, and then came writhing and rolling down the deep descent, and bit the dust at the base of the rock.

Led by Ambrose, who held on at a tremendous pace, and keeping as much as possible in the centre of the vale, the sailors made off towards the shore.

They were forced to pass through a narrow and dangerous gorge, wooded on either side, and here they were subject to a running fire of shots from the trees.

CHAPTER XXXIV.

MARK AMBROSE RECEIVES HIS DEATH WOUND.

SEVERAL poor fellows were wounded, and but for the devotion of their mess-mates, who, at great peril to themselves, bore them off, they must have been left upon the field, to be butchered in cold blood.

" Never mind," said Mr. Middleton, who himself had received an ugly wound in his arm, " bear up, jolly hearts, our turn will come next."

As soon as they had passed the gorge they breathed more freely.

The reserve was now seen rushing up.

Both parties cheered exultingly.

The first lieutenant walked up to Ambrose.

" Well done, my man," he said, with great heartiness; " this gallant action shall purchase for you a free pardon; but is the lady hurt?"

" No," returned Mark, quietly, " I think not, sir; but the sooner we get aboard the better."

" I am quite of your opinion," returned the lieutenant. " Our first care must be for the lady—did it come to a brush with the pirates?"

" Aye, sir, but we have as yet little to boast of in the way of glory."

" I suppose not; this is a very hornet's nest."

" Shall you leave a party of men on the island, sir?" asked Mr. Middleton.

" Mind your own business, sir," returned his superior officer, rather harshly.

" Ah!" sighed poor little Middleton, slinking back, " it's all very fine; but I shall be a first lieutenant some day, old boy."

" Mr. Middleton is wounded, sir," said the boatswain of the ' Fearless,' " touching his hat.

" You don't say so!" rejoined the lieutenant, in great concern. " My poor little fellow, and you did not mention that. You spoke so coolly; I am sorry that I answered with sharpness."

" Oh! sir!" returned the mid, in sublime indifference, " there's nothing to faint about; it was not worth mention."

But, nevertheless, he looked as if he were not unlikely to faint, for his cheek was ghastly pale, his blue lips twitched with pain, his left arm drooped and was covered with welling blood.

The lieutenant ordered a halt.

With many expressions of sympathy he proceeded to bandage the boy's wound with his own hands.

Mr. Middleton persisted that it was but a mere scratch, and indignantly rejected the offer of one of the men to carry him on his shoulders.

The mid seemed to contemplate his mishap, " to hug his sorrow and enjoy his pain," with ill-suppressed pride and self-glorification.

Pacing stoutly on, with the endurance of a young Spartan, by the side of Jack Rushton, he complimented him very patronizingly upon his valour and prowess, but implied delicately, "But, then, you see, you came off scatheless—*I* was wounded."

Jack smiled roguishly, and paid his tribute to merit in a very hearty style, and really felt an awakening regard for the gallant little mid—he had not liked him much at first, thought him rather too "bumptious"—a regard which afterwards developed in the warmest and most lasting friendship.

The party had now passed through the gorge, and emerged upon the summit of the cliffs that overhung the sea.

Here they paused for a rest, and took a bird's-eye view of land and main.

Far on the left was a high peak, which rose at the end of a long sandy promontory jutting out into the sea.

Off this point the pirate schooner—a long, low, rakish-looking craft— lay to, her sails furled.

A cloud of small boats, proas, and the like, were seen rowing towards her.

Even at that distance it could be seen that they were laden deep with casks and bales.

"The scoundrels are embarking!" cried the lieutenant.

"So much the better, yer honour," returned the boatswain, with a grin, " we shall have all the fun of a chase."

"And perhaps be outsailed."

"By such a lubber as that," growled the old salt, turning his quid; "smash me, yer honour, she's a rakish craft enough, and I'll warrant her a good sailer."

"Aye, it is time we were aboard."

"Hark!"

The report of a gun came booming over the heaving sea.

Then the "Fearless" was descried sailing grandly under pressure of canvas round another headland of the isle.

"Hurrah!" shouted the men.

"Aboard, my hearties!" cried the lieutenant. "We are signalled."

They were now passing down the rugged rockway which led to the beach.

Ambrose was in advance, still carrying Lady Marion in his arms, for no one seemed to venture upon asking him to relinquish his burden.

Jack Rushton came next, with Pomp and Tom Hawser.

Snap was gambolling on before.

Suddenly the dog stopped, crouched down upon his haunches, and uttered a savage growl.

The next moment, a hideous-looking black fellow, uttering a wild whoop, leaped over a rock, and struck a fierce blow with a gleaming creese at the bosom of the lady.

Mark interposed his own body.

"Ayah—yah—cuss buccra tief!" yelled the savage, making another plunge at Ambrose.

But Snap was at his throat in an instant.

Growling with deep ferocity, he dashed him back.

"It is that villain Matanza!" cried Jack.

But the black was now buried and struggling in the herbage with Snap.

Suddenly, a fearful yell rang along the cliffs.

Jack sprang upon a ledge of rock.

The dark body of the negro was seen whirling through the air, and Snap was struggling desperately up the slippery side of the almost perpendicular crag.

Jack turned away with a shudder.

A shout of rage and pity caused Jack to spring towards Mark.

The doomed man was half reclining upon a rock, surrounded by the whole of the party.

His head drooped, and his limbs quivered.

"Mark! Mark!" cried Jack, wildly seizing his hand; "you are wounded. The wretch has stabbed you!"

"Aye, lad; 'tis no matter; 'tis well," returned the poor fellow, turning his bloodshot eyes upon Lady Marion, whom the lieutenant was raising in his arms. "Lift her gently; ask pardon for me of her husband, my captain. Where are ye, lad? my eyes are dim—ha—so—let 'em bury me here. Don't take me aboard. Remember me when you get to Old England; re——"

He sank backwards, and swooned.

CHAPTER XXXV.

DEATH OF MARK AMBROSE.

MARK AMBROSE was lifted in the arms of his sympathising comrades, and softly borne to the boat.

He had evidently received his death wound, for his face wore that calm, fatal look which immediately precedes dissolution.

He opened his eyes and glared round him with a wild but conscious stare.

His guernsey was saturated with the red gushing life-tide, and his limbs hung limp and nerveless.

Ever to one point his rolling eyes wandered back, and fixed themselves with a yearning glance upon the frail and inanimate form of Lady Marion, who was now carried along by a couple of seamen.

Jack Rushton walked by his side, and, despite his manly nature, was so moved by the piteous spectacle that he sobbed like a girl.

As for poor Pomp, the simple fellow's grief was boundless, and vented itself in the most passionate outburst.

Even old Tom Hawser from time to time drew his sleeve across his eyes, and when a question was addressed to him answered only by a sigh or a groan.

"Cheer up, Mark," murmured our hero, "your wound is not mortal; the surgeons will save you yet, hearty; you must not, you shall not die."

Mark smiled faintly, and tried to speak, but the words fainted on his dying lips.

He was evidently suffering the keenest anguish; every nerve quivered convulsively, but he endured the pain with the stoic fortitude of a Red Indian at the stake.

"The cursed villains shall pay dearly for this!" exclaimed Mr. Archer, the first-lieutenant, as with bitter vehemence he shook his fist at the distant schooner, which was now crowding on all sail and getting under weigh.

The sorrowful party got into the boat, the wounded man was laid upon the gratings, his head pillowed upon the jackets which the men had thrown off with rough but kindly eagerness.

The insensible lady was supported in the lieutenant's arms, and the boat was shoved off.

Soon she was rocking under the bows of the " Fearless."

The unfortunate lovers were borne over the side.

The first to spring forward was Captain Varney.

The old man's face was ghastly pale and haggard, and he seemed about to sink upon the deck.

Archer caught him in his arms.

" Lady Marion—my wife—is she saved ? " gasped the captain, in a choking voice.

" Aye, sir ; by the heroism of this noble fellow," returned the lieutenant, solemnly, " who has sacrificed his own life for her sake."

" God forgive me ! " rejoined the captain, with sincere remorse, " I have wronged him cruelly."

He knelt by the side of his former rival and foe, and tenderly took his hand.

" Is it peace, Mark Ambrose ? " he whispered, softly. " Have I your pardon for the past ? "

" Aye, sir," returned Mark, faintly ; " I was most to blame."

Lady Marion was taken below, and, restoratives being applied, she soon recovered her senses.

Her first inquiry was for her pre-server ; and when the fatal news was gently conveyed to her she uttered a frantic shriek, and abandoned herself to a wordless despair.

Meanwhile Mark had been carried to the gun-room and laid in a hammock.

The surgeon attended to examine the wound. Jack Rushton stood by his side, and eagerly scanned his face, but could read no hope in his serious countenance.

" Is there no chance for him, sir ? " he asked, in a quivering voice, " none whatever ? "

" No, poor fellow, not the least in the world," returned the doctor, shaking his head ; " he has not half-an-hour to live."

" Aye, you say right, sir," Ambrose broke in, with startling clearness, " I am dying fast. I do not repine ; I have been guilty of a dark crime, and do not murmur at a just punishment. The sad story of my life will soon be brought to an end, and all I can hope for is that my sins may be forgiven and forgotten. Come hither, lad."

With a sickening qualm at his heart our hero placed his hand in his dying friend's clasp.

Mark clutched it feebly, and smiled with much tenderness and quietude.

" Hear my last words, lad," he said. " Till I met you in the Pirates' Lair, I thought my heart was dead; but your brave and kindly conduct revived the smouldering spark. My heart, long cold and desolate, warmed to ye, lad, with a father's love. I hungered for sympathy, and I found an object and a motive worth living for ; you were the object, because you pitied me, and dealt charitably with me, guilty wretch that I have been; the motive was to deliver you from the deadly perils that surrounded you. Do not let all my toil be thrown away! You will, no doubt, soon engage the pirate; you will volunteer to join the cutting-out party, and, in your fury at my loss, your eagerness to revenge me, you will throw away your life. Do not so, lad; I think I should rise from the deep sea—that I could not rest in my ocean grave— if I thought, now, that you would perish."

"Oh, Mark, you have taught me to hold my life most precious," sobbed Jack. "You have suffered and sacrificed all for its worthless sake, and I will preserve it with the coward's caution rather than you should have one anxious thought for me now. I have cost you too much already."

"'Tis well, lad, and so God for ever bless ye, and shield ye on sea and shore. There is one thing that would make death easy to me."

"Name it, Ambrose," said the captain, gently.

"She—Marion!" gasped the dying man, raising himself upon his arm with that strange, spasmodic power which often exerts itself in the last hour of failing life.

"My Marion!" he cried, fiercely; "for she was mine. As boy and girl we plighted troth together. Let me see her—alone—before I die."

"Your wish shall be gratified, Mark Ambrose," said Captain Varney. "Let all leave the gun-room. I will bring Marion hither."

"Ah! captain," sighed Ambrose, faintly, as he sank back on the pillow, "had you always been as kind and lenient with me, I should never have been either mutineer or pirate. Farewell, lad," he added, embracing our hero. "Remember your old friend, Mark, who shared all your perils in the Pirates' Lair."

Jack Rushton tried to answer; but, choked with sorrowful emotion, he could not speak.

Captain Varney led him from the room.

Pale as a spectre, and quivering like a leaf, Lady Marion stole softly down the companion stair, and crept into the berth in which the dying man lay.

Captain Varney and Jack instinctively retired; the others had already gone on deck.

They walked aft, and retired into the captain's cabin. Neither spoke. Varney seated himself, and, bending his head upon his breast, seemed to abandon himself to remorse and regret.

Jack hid his face upon the table and wept bitterly.

Suddenly a piercing shriek ran along the deck.

The captain and our hero started up in great alarm.

They rushed to the berth.

Lady Marion knelt beside the bed; Mark's long, heavy, black elf locks streamed over her shoulder; his arm drooped around her neck.

They gently disengaged the lady from his death-clasp.

He fell back, the rapture of repose impressed upon his cold, white, rigid face; his jaw fell, and his glassy eyes were fixed and spiritless; he was quite dead!

Captain Varney bore his fainting wife from the gun-room, and our hero, now that all was over, stood gazing upon the body of his friend with manly, tearless sorrow.

CHAPTER XXXVI.

THE CHASE OF THE PIRATES.

The excitement which prevailed amongst the crew of the "Fearless" was only equalled by their rage and thirst for vengeance upon the bloodstained wretches who had been the cause of so much misery.

The men aloft were crowding on every stitch of canvas, while on deck all was bustle and seeming confusion.

The drums and fifes beat to quarters, officers were shouting their orders, men were mustering at the guns, grape and canister were being deftly handed up from below, and the gallant frigate bore bravely on under a cloud of canvas.

The marines were filing aft and gathering on the quarter-deck, while the armourers were distributing hand-pikes and cutlasses to the men selected for the cutting-out party.

Captain Varney and the first lieutenant walked the side, and from time to time the officers turned their glasses eagerly in the direction of the pirate schooner, which now appeared skimming along the sky-line.

Jack stood by the breech of the long gun, and, with burning heart, watched the chase; he panted for vengeance, but did not forget the promise that he had made to Mark, feeling that it was his duty to take care of that life which his friend had died to save.

"Keep a good full!" shouted the lieutenant; "the fellow travels at a spanking rate, and lies close to the wind."

"Aye, aye, sir," rejoined Tom Hawser; "but this yere vessel didn't sail on a Friday, that's one mercy, and you'll see, sir, as we shall overhaul the rascal yet."

"Yes, I think we're too much for him," rejoined the lieutenant.

The men watched the chase with breathless suspense.

The wind had freshened to half a gale, and the ship was sailing at a tremendous rate under heavy press of canvas.

Every now and then the brave tars would start and look up at the bellying sails and straining cordage, as a crackling sound aloft aroused a fear in their hearts lest something had "gone," and that the rate of sailing would be slackened.

Still the pirate schooner continued to draw a-head.

The lieutenant fretted and fumed with impatience.

The men turned their quids, growled their disgust, and stared with starting eyes at the flying chase.

"Hang me, if we're not falling astern, and to leeward, Mr. Middleton," said the second lieutenant.

"Aye, sir," returned that plucky little Briton; "but look, sir, the wind has veered."

"So it has, by George; now we shall have him!"

"Hurrah!" responded the men, with hearty union, "Hurrah!"

After a long and fierce chase, during which the two vessels had exchanged running shots, the "Fearless" over-reached the schooner, which hauled in her main braces and bore to.

The crew of the "Fearless" at this sight uttered a stirring cheer as the noble frigate ran alongside the schooner, and the two ships lay stern to stern.

"Take good aim, men," cried the first-lieutenant, springing down from the main gangway, and drawing his sword. "We'll give them one more raking broadside, and then we'll cut them out by the board!"

"Eigh, sir!" shrieked Pomp, rushing up to the officer and flinging himself upon his knees before him, "pray, sar, mind what yo go do."

"What does the black lubber mean?" growled one of the gunners.

"De lilly gal, sar," cried Pompey, to the lieutenant, pointing eagerly at the pirate-ship, "lilly Missee Transom—Missee Nellie, sar; de cuss pirate kill she if yo not take care."

"Just heaven! I had forgotten her," cried the lieutenant. "Hold hard, my lads; where is the captain?"

"Here, Mr. Archer," returned Sir Richard, stepping up the companion ladder of the main hatchway. "Has the villain struck?"

"Not he, sir; look at his bunting," returned the lieutenant.

A large red flag, embroidered with the figures of a skull and a sword, floated from the peak of the schooner.

The whole of the crew of the pirate ship, which was very numerous, were crowded upon the deck.

The most perfect order and silence prevailed amongst them.

"The impudent scoundrel," cried the captain of the "Fearless;" "but we'll have no palaver with him. Give him another broadside, lieutenant, and blow him off the face of the water."

"But stop, captain; what are we to do about the child, poor Transom's daughter, whom, no doubt, he has aboard; you may depend upon it that the blackguard will murder her if we are too precipitate."

"Well reminded, Mr. Archer," said the captain, aghast with perplexity. "What shall we do in the matter?"

"See! the rascal has signalled that he wants to speak with us," interrupted the lieutenant.

"I should like to give him his answer from the throats of our guns! But we must hear what he has to say, for the child's sake," replied the captain.

The ships now lay so near each other that from either deck words could be distinguished.

Suddenly Don Pablo sprang upon the lee bulwarks forward.

The pirates brandished their weapons and uttered a yelling cheer.

"Surrender, you villain!" shouted the captain of the "Fearless," shaking his fist at the daring outlaw.

"Never!" returned Don Pablo, with a laugh, as he pointed his sword at the red flag fluttering over his head. "And beware what you do, senor el capitan; your next shot may pierce the bosom of this little one."

And he held Nellie up in his arms.

"Coward! miscreant!" shouted the captain of the "Fearless." "You would not harm an innocent little thing like that? Hark ye; if you will send her on board this vessel, I will give you my word of honour, as an English officer, that you shall have an hour's law to repair your damages and get under weigh!"

"Bueno!" said the pirate, curtly. "And what more, senor capitan?"

"Why, we will heave to, and give you a chance of out-sailing us. But, mark this, if we come up with you again, you must expect no quarter," said Captain Varney.

The pirate laughed scornfully, and placed the child on his shoulder.

At that moment, as he stood upon a carronade, in his rich gold-bedizened dress, his swart face aglare with ferocious determination, a bright-coloured bandanna silk kerchief fluttering from his brow, his naked sabre flashing in his hand, and the poor trembling little one cowering upon his broad shoulder, he would have formed a fine model for some romantic painting.

"Your answer!" cried the English captain.

"Carrajo! I must have better terms than that," returned the pirate, with a sneer, "or I will cut the girl to pieces before your eyes. I'll have no trifling; I will leave the child on the island of Sanpan in charge of the Indians, where you can send for her at the end of three days. Meantime, you must tack about and return to the port you hailed from, and the child shall be surrendered to no one but my followers, Gonzalves and the maid Juanita, whom you must send to fetch her."

"You unconscionable scoundrel!"

"Muy bein; you have my offer; I give you five minutes to decide whether you will accept it; at the end of that time, if you are inhuman enough to refuse it, I will kill the girl, fire the magazine, and blow the schooner into the air."

The English officers were confounded.

They knew not what to do; for they felt assured that the determined villain would not hesitate an instant in carrying out his desperate resolve.

Jack Rushton, Tom Hawser, and the brave little middy, Mr. Middleton, were gathered in a group, watching the scene, and listening to the colloquy in breathless suspense.

Snap was crouching at our hero's feet, watching every movement of the pirates, and snarling fiercely.

Suddenly Jack was startled by a whisper in his ear.

"'Tand back, Massa Rushton."

He stepped aside.

It was Pompey who had spoken.

The negro stood poising a musket in his hand.

He raised it to his shoulder.

Flash! Bang!

The next instant Don Pablo reeled backwards and gripped at the ratlines.

"Maldito! Traditones! Moy picado! Curses! Traitors! I am struck!" cried the pirate chief.

His cry was echoed by a deafening yell of rage and consternation from his felon crew.

But where was the child?

At the same instant that the bullet had entered the breast of Don Pablo, he had thrown the child forwards.

With a loud scream, she flew through the air, and plashed into the water.

A terrible shout ran along the decks of the frigate.

Every eye was turned to the place where the little one was struggling in the foamy swell.

Over the bulwarks sprang the trusty Snap, and was soon paddling through the foam.

Overboard sprang Jack, and Tom Hawser immediately leaped after him.

"Hurrah! hurrah!" shouted the British tars.

Pompey had hold of the child, and was seen scrambling up the main-chains, and then he ducked through a porthole, closely followed by Jack, and Tom Hawser, and Snap, whom our hero lugged by the scurf of his neck.

Again and again the delighted seamen made the air ring with their hearty huzzahs.

"Boarders, away there!" cried the captain, waving his sword.

Then arose the deafening din of the cannonade and musket shots, and the good vessel quivered beneath the recoil of her thundering guns.

On to the bloodstained deck of the doomed pirate vessel poured a hundred fierce assailants.

Jack and Tom Hawser, with the gallant little mid, led the van.

In the middle of the deck lay Don Pablo, his head pillowed upon the faithful bosom of the devoted Inez, who kissed his pale brow, murmured her frantic supplications to the Holy Virgin, and seemed blind to every object but her dying husband, deaf to every sound but his death groans.

The pirates fought like demons, and long and loud was the hellish uproar.

Blood ran in pools along the deck.

No one attempted to molest the wretched woman who was soothing the dying agonies of him she had loved not wisely but too well.

Suddenly Don Pablo raised himself upon his arm, and glared round with dying eyes.

"Vengeance!" he shouted. "Fight, comrades! Down with the English bloodhounds. Triad, pendejos! fire the magazine! Ay, dios; yo muero, Inez mi querida; Idio, Inez—love; adios, Ad——"

He fell back stone dead, and, with a piercing shriek, the poor girl swooned upon his breast.

The battle raged madly.

"Save the senora!" cried Jack, to the men nearest to him. "Do not let her perish."

"Overboard, all of ye!" yelled the lieutenant. "The pirate devils have got to the magazine; we shall all be blown to pieces."

Breathless and bloodstained, the men scrambled back over the bulwarks, and poured on to the deck of the " Fearless."

Jack, and his friend, the mid, were the last to leave the ship.

They tried to save Donna Inez, but in vain; they lingered till the last moment, and only escaped death by a hair's breadth.

Then come a thunderous roar, that bellowed in prolonged echoes through the deep hills of the distant island.

The air was inflamed with a burning light, and the sea strewn with fragments of human bodies and the debris of the shattered schooner.

"It is all over," gasped our hero, leaning faintly against a carronade, and grasping his friend Middleton's hand. "My poor messmates, and my brave, though misguided, friend, Mark Ambrose, are avenged! So perish every bloodstained pirate on the high seas!"

*   *   *   *   *

Our story is ended; and with a few parting words we must bid our young readers adieu, but not without giving them some account of the after career of the leading characters in our drama.

Jack Rushton returned to England, and, as may well be imagined, was most joyfully received by his mother. He afterwards obtained a commission, through the interest of Captain Varney, as midshipman aboard the " Fearless," and Tom Haswer also entered the same vessel.

Jack and Middleton became fast friends, and their friendship remained firm and unshadowed through life.

Our hero's promotion was rapid, and at the age of twenty-five he retired from the service a post-captain.

Sir Richard Varney did not long survive the events we have recorded.

Lady Varney never married again; she adopted the orphaned Nellie Transom, and took the faithful Pompey into her service; the trusty Snap also remained with his little mistress, and lived long her pet companion.

At the age of nineteen Nellie married Captain Rushton, and the first child she bore him was christened Mark, in remembrance of our hero's old and hapless friend.

And now if there be any of our boy readers who have felt an inclination to sympathise with or admire " dashing rovers " and " bold buccaneers " let him reflect on the dark deeds of the false, cruel, and bloodthirsty Don Pablo, and recall the perils and sufferings of our hero, Jack Rushton, during the eventful time which he spent " ALONE IN THE PIRATES' LAIR."

THE END.